Roger Jackson

CRADLE OF THE DEAD

BLOOD BOUND BOOKS

Cradle of the Dead Copyright © 2014 by Roger Jackson
Dark Waves Copyright © 2014 by Simon Kearns
All rights reserved

ISBN 978-1-940250-10-6

Artwork by Andrej Bartulovic

Interior Layout by Lori Michelle

Printed in the United States of America

First Edition

Visit us on the web at:
www.bloodboundbooks.net

Also from Blood Bound Books:

400 Days of Oppression by Wrath James White
Habeas Corpse by Nikki Hopeman
Mother's Boys by Daniel I. Russell
Fallow Ground by Michael James McFarland
Loveless by Dev Jarrett
The Sinner by K. Trap Jones
The Return by David A. Riley
Knuckle Supper by Drew Stepek
Sons of the Pope by Daniel O'Connor
Dolls by KJ Moore
At the End of All Things by Stony Graves
The Black Land by MJ Wesolowski

CHAPTER ONE

"How MUCH FURTHER?" Paul Wren asked.

"Not far," Markham told him. He twisted the wheel to avoid clipping yet another sudden rise in the empty, uneven road. "Couple of miles."

Wren nodded, though Markham kept his eyes on the road unrolling ahead of them, watching the headlights play jaggedly over the scattered islands of spoiled snow. Wren was glad of Markham's concentration. It had been almost an hour since they had seen another car, but it was Christmas Eve, and Wren wasn't about to discount the possibility of some idiot coming back late from an office party or something, taking a clever little shortcut that would bring them hurtling out of the dark toward a head-on collision. The road was narrow, flanked on both sides by a great tangle of trees, and there would be no way to avoid one.

Thankful for Markham's focus or not, the truth was that the silence that had unfolded in the car since they had left the motorway was getting on his nerves, but it was a weird thing—the nearer they got to Alderville, the less he felt like talking. He almost considered clicking the radio back on, but knew that all it would offer would be either the same yuletide tunes he'd been hearing in the shops since the beginning of November, or dusty-voiced clergy discussing the meaning of Christmas. Markham's small selection of CDs in the glove compartment wasn't much better, one collection of mournful country ballads after another but still, the silence gnawed at him, giving him too much space to think.

He almost wished that Vince would start screaming again.

He jabbed his thumb in the direction of the boot. "He's gone pretty quiet back there," Wren said. "You don't reckon he's croaked, do you?"

"If he's dead then so are we," Markham said grimly. "Baxter wants a little chat first."

Wren hadn't asked what kind of trouble Vince was in. It was the Unwritten Rule of being in Adam Baxter's employ, and it tied in nicely with Wren's personal philosophy of keeping his eyes open and his mouth shut. Not that he wasn't curious. You didn't get the word to stick a man you worked with—an *associate*, as Baxter would say—in the boot of a car without wondering what the poor bastard had done to deserve it.

He looked out through the passenger window, seeing little beyond his own pallid reflection. There wasn't a lot out there to see. The trees were blurring past them like smoke now, and beyond the trees there were no streetlights, no vehicles, no buildings save what had looked like an abandoned farmhouse maybe ten miles back. Nothing more than acres of snow-dusted land vanishing into the black horizon, an unchanging terrain that was cold and dead and somehow lunar in its emptiness.

Suddenly Markham's mobile began twittering at them from its perch on the dash. Markham glanced sourly at the display and silenced it without answering. He unclipped the phone and slipped it into his jacket, but not before Wren had noted the Caller ID: *Home.*

"What's up?" he asked Markham evenly after a moment or two. "Trouble in Paradise?"

Markham hesitated before replying, "It's nothing. Just that we've got the Out-Laws coming round for Christmas dinner tomorrow, and it's causing a bit of friction, you know."

"Yeah, I can imagine," Wren said. He'd met Markham's wife only once, months ago. Her name was Susan. Wren guessed she'd been a bit of a stunner, back in her day, but now her features were hard and lined behind the cosmetic

war-paint, her hair a bottle-blonde. She had been civil
enough, though the stark distrust of him in her eyes told
Wren that she knew what kind of men her husband worked
with, and the kind of man who paid his wages.

"Her mum's all right," Markham went on. "It's her old
man who's the pain in the arse. He's a right snobby sod, well
into opera and Shakespeare and all that. Doesn't think I'm
posh enough for his precious little girl."

Wren shrugged. "Yeah, well, no-one's ever going to
accuse you of being a culture vulture, are they?"

"I'm fucking well cultured, me," Markham said sharply,
though Wren could see that he was trying not to smile. "I
read that *Fifty Shades* book, well, bits of it . . . I'm interested
in European Cinema—"

"German porn does *not* count as European Cinema."
Wren laughed, and after a moment Markham was laughing
too.

"I can't be bothered with all that Christmas bollocks,
anyway," Markham told him. "It's just another fucking
money-making racket. Christ, it's bad enough with Susie
wanting her fucking designer stuff, I'm just glad we don't
have any—"

He broke off. Stared at the road, his hands suddenly
tighter than they needed to be on the wheel. Knowing
Markham as he did, Wren knew that the sudden silence was
the nearest to an apology he was ever going to get. But they
had worked together for five, maybe six years now, been
through a lot of shit together, and each of them knew that
silence was the only apology needed.

"How are you?" Markham said after a moment or two.
"Both of you."

"We're fine." An image flashed into his mind. The half-
painted nursery. It had been six weeks since Nikki—since
they—had lost the baby, and still Wren couldn't bring himself
to paint over the delicate pink that covered two of the four
walls. The task defeated him day after day, like sleep, like

enjoying the football again, like getting through a single fucking day without him and Nikki either sitting in silence or screaming at each other. "Just getting on with things, y'know."

He should have been home, but this—the unlit road, Markham complaining about his father-in-law, the body in the boot—this was easier.

Gradually, the border of trees was thinning, replaced by glittering lawns of snow broken here and there by an explosion of untamed topiary or the remnants of a long dead rosebush erupting from the whiteness like the gnarled hands of ghost-train skeletons. The road curved right and they followed it, until their path was blocked by a pair of tall iron gates fixed like prison bars into the perimeter wall encircling Alderville's grounds.

They stopped. In the blaze of the headlights Wren could see that the gates were secured by a thick galvanised chain, tarnished now by the elements but clearly newer than the gates themselves, looping through the bars and sealed with a padlock the size of his fist.

"There you go." Markham drew something from his jacket and passed it to Wren. A long, iron key. "Since it's your first time here you can have the honour of letting us in."

"Thanks," Wren said doubtfully. "That honour wouldn't have anything to do with the fact that it's fucking freezing out there, would it?"

"Not a bit of it." Markham smiled. "On you go."

Shaking his head, Wren unbuckled his seatbelt and got out. The cold night hit him straight away, and he zipped up his jacket as he hurried around the front of the car to the gates. He took hold of the padlock—the metal was rimed with frost, and cold enough to numb his fingertips as he inserted the key and sprung the lock. He slipped the padlock into his pocket and uncoiled the chain from around the bars, taking a moment to look at Alderville through them.

Decades ago, it had been some sort of psychiatric

hospital, but to Wren's eyes the shape of it looked more like a mansion or stately home, like fucking Wayne Manor or something. Even from this short distance, Wren could make out nothing of the building's features. It stood lightless at every window, framed against the night sky like a house carved from shadow. Another car was already parked outside. Baxter's car. He glanced back at his own transport and saw that Markham was speaking on his mobile. The light from the phone showed Wren that the man's brows had drawn together like thunderheads, and that his sentences were brief. It occurred to Wren that Markham might be doing something that *he* should be doing, calling home, and so he took a minute or so longer than he needed to in opening the gates.

But when he turned back to the car, ready to guide Markham through the gates, he saw that the other man had finished his call and was beckoning to him.

"That was Baxter," Markham told him when he opened the car door and leaned in. "He wants to get started. Gotta get home for midnight mass or something. You know what a pillar of the community he is."

Wren held up the chain he still carried. "What about the gates?"

"Leave 'em." Markham shook his head. "Dunno who the fuck is gonna disturb us out here anyway. Come on."

Wren coiled the chain in the footwell and got in. Markham took them through the gates slowly, then picked up speed as they moved along the driveway.

"The fella who ran Alderville was a German," Markham informed him suddenly, and Wren wondered dismally if this was a route back to the subject of Markham's European film collection. "He owned it as well, if I remember rightly. Christ, he must have made a packet. A lot of rich bastards used to have their loony relatives locked up there, back when that sort of thing was a bit of a scandal, you know? I suppose people back then weren't as understanding about having a nutcase in the family as they are now."

Wren raised an eyebrow, waiting to see if his friend was attempting some sort of irony, but . . . no. It seemed as though Harry Markham's map to the Land of Political Correctness was upside down again.

"They kept them locked up here out of the way their whole lives," Markham went on. Alderville loomed beyond the windscreen. "Even buried 'em here, nice and tidy. The cemetery's over there." He looked briefly to his right, and without thinking about it, Wren followed his glance with one of his own, though he could see nothing more than the snowy ground receding into blackness.

Suddenly the car caught another bump in the road—from the boot, Wren heard Eddie yelp.

"He's still breathing, then," he said.

"Lucky for us," Markham replied. He sighed. "Christ, I'm dying for a cigarette."

"You could have had one on the way," Wren told him. He'd given up smoking about six months ago, the weekend after Nikki had told him she was pregnant. She had already stopped before then, but now, she was back on a pack a day, sometimes more. "It wouldn't have bothered me."

Markham shook his head. "This is Susie's car, and she's gone all holier-than-thou since she started on the patches. If I lit up in here, Vince wouldn't be the only one that's not gonna need a *TV Guide* for Boxing Day." He smiled ruefully. They were almost at the building's main door now. "I'd be safer in this place with Doctor Von Psycho."

"What happened to the German?" Wren asked him. "The doctors, the patients . . . where did they all end up?"

Markham shrugged. "I dunno. Baxter could tell you, he's like a fucking walking Wikipedia about this place." He smiled. "He did say something once, though. Me and McKenzie had brought some kid here that Baxter wanted taking out, and before we do him, Baxter starts going on about some brain experiments the docs were doing here back in the old days, real fucked-up stuff by the sound of it, and about how it was a crime they got closed down before they could finish their work." His smile broadened. "You know what Baxter's like though, he loves to build up the drama before a kill."

"Jesus," Wren muttered. "This place gets more Hammer horror by the minute."

Markham brought the car to a stop. "Wait until you see what's inside," he said.

CHAPTER TWO

THEY GOT OUT of the car. Markham strolled around to the boot to get Vince, but Wren hesitated a moment, taking his first good look at the infamous Alderville.

Now that he was closer, the building itself seemed unremarkable, quite unlike the gothic horror of towers and gargoyles that his mind had woven from all the talk of killings and torture. Three floors high, it was austere and unwelcoming. Beneath the vaulted, snow-heavy roof, Alderville wore its weathered brickwork like armour, a crumbling facade punctuated only by the great main door and the narrow windows blinded by their cataracts of rusting mesh. There was more snow dusting the worn stone steps that led up to the door, and now Wren noted two sets of tracks imprinted into the white. Baxter was here, and one other—probably that prick, McKenzie.

The longer Wren looked up at it though, standing in the dark with the chill sinking into his bones, the more a sense of disquiet seeped into him also. There *was* something troubling about Alderville, something elemental, as though everything around them, the cold, the dark, the howling black night itself, was bleeding from its decaying brickwork.

But then Markham was calling his name, and he turned and headed to where the other man stood waiting, at the back of the car.

"Here," he said. In one hand he held a heavy, rubber-encased torch. The other hand was tugging an automatic pistol from his belt. "Cop this."

Wren looked down at the gun, surprised. He jerked his chin at the boot. "He won't be any trouble. He's scared."

"He's fucking terrified." Markham smiled thinly. "That's why I'm giving you the gun. Come on, take it. I'm freezing my nuts off out here."

Shrugging, Wren took the weapon from Markham's hand and angled it toward the rear of the vehicle. The other man had a point, he supposed. If Vince *was* spooked enough to make a break for it, then it would be better to dissuade him now than to have to go chasing after him through a crumbling, pitch-black boneyard.

Markham snapped the boot open and stepped back. "Out," he said.

"Markham?" Vince's voice was small, hesitant, and a little croaky from the screaming. "Harry, what's going on? Where—"

"Out, I said," Markham snapped. From where he stood, Wren couldn't see Vince, only hear him, and for one lunatic moment this whole scene felt wrong, as though he were watching some surreal ventriloquist act with Markham throwing his own voice into the boot. He didn't like it and moved in a little nearer.

"You've got about three seconds, Vince." Markham lifted the torch and clicked it on, illuminating their captive. Vince was in there all right, trembling, his body curved into a foetal coil. He wasn't a big man, five-seven tops and scrawny, but even so he was squeezed in there pretty tight, his knees tucked up against his chest. How Vince might fit into the cramped space wasn't something that Wren had really considered—in his experience of transporting bodies in boots, you could pretty much break them into any shape you needed.

Stiffly, Vince swung one of his legs over the lip of the boot. He wasn't wearing any shoes, Wren noticed, only a pair of thin dove-grey socks. As Vince shifted his other leg, Markham cursed and snatched impatiently at his captive's shirt, yanking him out of the boot. Vince yelped and tumbled to the snowy ground.

Markham slammed the boot shut. He glared down at Vince. "On your feet."

Awkwardly, Vince obeyed, his muscles clearly still in knots after his confinement. He stood there shivering, his unprotected feet buried in the snow, hugging himself against the night's chill. In spite of the cold, great circles of sweat darkened the underarms of his powder-blue shirt; tatters of steam rose from his brow. His eyes were narrowed into slits, blinded by the torchlight, but they widened as he registered first that his colleague Paul Wren was pointing a handgun at his face, swiftly followed by the realisation of where they had brought him.

"Alderville . . ."

"That's right, Vince." Markham reached out and placed a firm hand on the smaller man's shoulder. "And you've been here enough times to know that we can make tonight last as long as we want. So have the sense not to fuck us about, eh?"

"Alderville . . ." Vince said again, streamers of pale air uncoiling from his trembling lips. "I . . . Harry, I don't understand, Jesus Christ, I haven't done anything, I haven't—"

"Baxter says different, and I've got a mortgage to pay," Markham said neutrally. "You know the score, Vince. It's just business."

Vince turned to face him, shaking his head. "Business," he repeated numbly. "Markham . . . Harry, we're mates, we—"

"Come on now." His tone was light, conversational, nothing to get Vince too excited, but Wren could see how Markham's eyes were fixed on Vince's, looking for that little spark of blind panic that would make Vince run or throw a random, abortive punch that, if the gun got involved, would mean trouble for all of them. After all, Baxter wanted his chat.

"Business is business," Markham was saying. "It's like that story about Scrooge, you know, the one that's on telly every Christmas. He's a miserable, tight-fisted old bastard, never gives anyone a break. Then he gets his ghosts, and one of 'em shows him the future, and he's dead, and all the people who he's fucked over through the years are jumping for joy. But then—and here's the moral, Vince . . . " Markham smiled. "Old Scrooge changes his ways, buys presents, throws a bit of cash around, and all the people that were dancing on his grave before the adverts suddenly wanna be his best mate. You understand what I'm saying here, don't you?"

Vince shook his head. "No, I—"

Markham held up his hand to quiet him, nodding sagely. "The moral of that story, Vince, and this one too, is that every man has his price. Do we have an understanding?"

Vince just stared at him, his eyes wide, his mouth like a smoking bullet hole. Markham flashed a smile at Wren that Wren took as, *There you go . . . fuckin' Culture Vulture or what?* He managed to return the smile, briefly, though his face felt suddenly numb with more than the cold and the smile felt sick and bitter on his lips.

Markham turned Vince around so he faced Alderville and gave him a little shove up the steps. Wren followed. The door at the head of the steps was rusted iron, and as they reached it Wren heard two, no, three heavy bolts being thrown open on the other side. After a moment the door swung inward— Wren had half expected the traditional horror movie screech of tortured hinges, but the door opened smoothly enough. He supposed the hinges saw too much use to fully seize up; by all accounts Baxter's little jaunts to Alderville were becoming more and more frequent.

The door opened fully, and a moment later Zach McKenzie appeared in the doorway.

There was something about McKenzie that had gotten under Wren's skin almost from the moment that Markham had introduced them perhaps six months ago in a back room of the Mariner's Tavern. They might have been friends—they had gone to the same school, albeit a year or so apart, had drank in the same pubs, knew some of the same people. Lots of common ground, but Wren saw something sly and fake in McKenzie's dark, narrow eyes. There was a honed affability to him that never quite rang true, something that always conjured for Wren a phrase his father had used when ranting about certain politicians: *Smiling Assassin.*

The truth was though, McKenzie never really smiled as such. He *smirked*, an arrogant upturn of his thin lips that rarely, if ever, revealed his teeth. Wren suspected that if he ever actually saw them that they would be small and neat and a little too white, and that the temptation to punch them into enamel splinters would be near irresistible.

Fortunately, he and McKenzie hadn't actually worked that much together, mostly the occasional bit of intimidation to hush up some local chatter about Baxter's business interests. The last time had been about a month ago, that incident with—

Wren's stomach tightened. The last time had been the incident with the girl, the one with the butterfly tattoo.

"All right, lads?" McKenzie said. Though he was still within the relative shelter of the doorway, he was stamping his feet and beating his gloved hands together to fend off the chill. "What's the hold up? You know the big fella doesn't like to be kept waiting."

Markham shook his head. "No hold up." He was smiling too, and his voice was pitched in the same neutral tone he'd used with Vince, but Wren could see it clearly enough from the way Markham's spine had stiffened. He didn't care for McKenzie's company anymore than Wren did. "Just a few last-minute nerves. All sorted."

McKenzie glanced down at Vince's once dove-grey socks—they were almost black now, completely soaked. "Yeah, well . . . I can see how he might have cold feet." He reached out and pinched Vince's cheek. "Cheer up, Vincey," he cooed. "It's Christmastime, there's no need to be afraid." Then, shrugging amiably, added, "Well, not apart from the boss wanting your guts for tinsel, anyway."

Markham had clamped one of his big hands around the crook of Vince's elbow, and now he pulled the smaller man a little nearer to him, almost protectively, Wren thought.

"Like you said, *Zachary*," he said, his eyes hard, his voice a little less even than before. "Mr Baxter doesn't like to wait."

McKenzie stared at him for a moment or two, his smirk still in place, then stepped back and gestured through the black doorway. "Okay," he said. "Come on in."

Markham stepped through the door, tugging Vince with him—Vince glanced back around at Wren, desperation in his red-rimmed eyes. McKenzie's pinch had left an angry little crescent on Vince's cheek, Wren saw, its lividness emphasising how pale Vince was; perhaps it was the moonlight, but Wren thought he might have been turning blue.

Then they were gone, through the doorway. McKenzie watched them go in then turned back to Wren, his smile actually a smile for once, displaying a row of neat white teeth that, yes, Wren did feel like shattering. "You not joining us then, Wren? You're invited to the party too, y'know." And then he too withdrew into the darkness, leaving Wren alone, standing in the shadow of Alderville, its cold aura seeming to numb him from the heart out.

"*Bastard*," Wren whispered. Seeing McKenzie tonight, being reminded of Tattoo Girl, it was just the last thing he needed. He wished he'd taken a minute or two to speak to Nikki before he'd left tonight, just to tell her that he would be home ASAP, just to say *something*, but he hadn't, he'd just left her in the house alone with a box full of Christmas decorations that he'd brought down from the attic yesterday and would put back up there tomorrow.

Wren looked down at the gun in his hand, suddenly repulsed by its cold, dead weight, as though he were holding some extracted tumour. He wished he could just throw it away right now, throw it as far as he could into the dark and walk away.

Disgusted, he tucked the gun into his belt and followed the others inside.

The main door led into a narrow, arched corridor, its floor tiled with monochrome diamond shapes. Wren could see that much by the moonlight, at least until McKenzie closed and bolted the door behind them. McKenzie had drawn a torch from somewhere inside his overcoat, but even combined with the beam from Markham's light it did little to dispel the gloom, and Wren found himself relying on every sense but sight to get a feel for his surroundings.

It felt no warmer in here than it had outside, he noted. Maybe there was a broken window or shattered skylight ahead, but the elements were definitely intruding from somewhere. As the group edged forward, gusts of cold swept past him in mournful whispers.

Ventilation or not though, the air was stale and dead, the musk of forced caskets and invaded crypts. It was coarse somehow, textured with dust. After just a few feet, he could feel it settling in his hair, seeking his eyes, silting his teeth and tongue. Particles swirled and ebbed in the torch beams, as if they were explorers in a snowglobe.

After a minute or two the corridor opened up into a larger space, much larger by the way the resonance of their combined footsteps changed. There was a little more light in here, too; at first Wren mistook it for his vision rebooting itself to cope with the gloom, but yes, there was some moonlight filtering through the dirt and the mesh of three broad, high windows on the far side of the room. It didn't show him much, but he guessed that they had reached some kind of entrance hall.

A large wooden desk stood to his left, its wide sheet of blotting paper thick with dust. Next to it, bizarrely, was one of those tall IV drip stands, jaundiced plastic tubes encircling its length like vines. An empty plastic bag hung from its apex, withered and drained, and in the thin light it looked to Wren almost as if it might have been a shrunken head, a tribal warning or one of Adam Baxter's sick trophies. There was more random furniture and equipment scattered around the chamber. Two rusting beds on wheels and their disintegrating mattresses, a door, torn from its hinges and abandoned against one wall, even a big leather couch, dusty and unravelling at the seams.

On the other side of the room, a wide iron staircase sprouted from the tiled floor and ascended to the next level, a kind of windowed gallery bordered by an ornate iron railing. Wren saw that Baxter was coming down to meet them, his footsteps echoing on the gridwork steps.

He was a tall, powerfully-built man, as stark and imposing a shape as Alderville itself. His customary dark suit and the heavy, charcoal-grey overcoat only added to his bulk. From this distance, ten feet or so, his eyes were little more than hard chips of reflected torchlight, but Wren could see his smile, a slice of white in the dark, and saw that in its own sick way that smile was genuinely, horribly welcoming.

As they drew nearer though, Wren realised that Baxter really *did* remind him of Alderville. There was something about how the torchlight turned his cropped blond hair almost white, like fake snow atop his heavy, thick set features, and how his eyes were as caged and unreadable as the meshed windows. Even the shade and hard lines of his overcoat all conspired to remake him in the image of Alderville's exterior, as though he'd spent so much time in its thrall that he'd come to resemble its outer shell, like a dog said to look like its master. Wren found himself wondering if, with enough blood on his hands, a killer might come to mirror his killing ground.

The notion struck him as both ludicrous and terrifying, but there was no time to dwell on it, because suddenly Baxter's smile was gone and he was running, charging at them like a bull, some vicious, guttural sound rising from his throat.

"Fuckin' hell," Markham said, managing to sound both surprised and dismayed in the same breath as he leapt gracelessly to one side.

Wren's hand instinctively went to the gun at his belt, and stayed there—he saw where Baxter's momentum was taking him, and it wasn't in his direction.

Vince saw Baxter hurtling forward, his feet stamping up great clouds of dust and the tails of his overcoat fanning out behind him, and began a shocked, childlike yell that Baxter silenced with a hard, back-handed slap that hooked the smaller man off his feet. Vince executed a clumsy mid-air pirouette and hit the tiled floor in a tangle of arms and legs, releasing a harsh, pained grunt.

Markham swung his torch beam around to cover Vince as Baxter moved to stand over him, breathing hard. "Get that fucking rat out of my sight," he said between gasps. "I'll deal with him soon enough."

"I got him," McKenzie said, hurrying forward. He hooked his forearm beneath one of Vince's armpits, hauling him unsteadily upright. Vince's wet socks slid about on the tiles, but somehow McKenzie kept him on his feet. He smiled—*assassin*—and whispered something in Vince's ear. The other man recoiled, but McKenzie just laughed and drew him off into the shadows.

Baxter stood with his back to them, his head down, his broad shoulders rising and falling as he worked on getting his composure back. After a moment or two he straightened and turned to face them. His hand was reaching up to fix his tie, pulled crooked by his charge, but after a second's consideration he just tugged it down to half-mast and unbuttoned his shirt collar.

"Markham . . . Wren." He nodded at them in turn. The smile was back, no warmer than it had been before. "You're late."

"Yep, sorry 'bout that." Markham shrugged. "Traffic was murder."

"I understand," Baxter said coolly. "I have an appointment later tonight but it's fine. Everything's in place here anyway, we'll just have to proceed a little faster than planned."

He crossed to where Wren stood and placed a hand on his shoulder. "I want you to know how much I appreciate you joining us tonight, Paul," he said. Hearing Baxter address Wren by his forename sounded strange to him. Only Nikki and his parents ever used it.

"I know this must be a difficult time for you and Nicola," Baxter went on. He shook his head reflectively. "I swear if anything ever happened to one of my girls . . . well, I don't know what I'd do."

There was a short, awkward pause between them, demanding some kind of response from Wren. "It's fine," he said at last. "Nikki's fine."

Baxter nodded, smiling. "I'll have you back with her before midnight. I promise." He stepped away from Wren, swinging his arm in a wide arc. "So . . . what do you make of my little sanctuary?"

Wren glanced around at the cold, dark chamber. "Lots of space, plenty of character," he said evenly. "Needs brightening up, though. Maybe a couple of paintings or something."

Baxter laughed, nodding. "Oh, it's got character, all right. This place . . . " He tilted his head back slightly, staring into the darkness above them. "It's more than bricks and mortar. Close your eyes and you can feel it, almost taste it. The history. The tears. The madness."

Wren frowned. All he could taste in this hellhole was damp and decay, and he didn't need to hear Adam Baxter going all Colonel Kurtz about it. He glanced across at Markham, who merely shrugged and pulled his cigarettes out from inside his jacket.

"Sometimes . . . " Baxter moved across to one of the windows—the glass was frosted with filth and sealed with mesh, almost opaque, but Wren didn't need to see through it to know what the view would be. "Sometimes I come here alone, even when there's no business to take care of, just for the peace."

Wren glanced over at Markham, though Harry wasn't looking at him. He stood with a cigarette hanging from his lips, his hands patting his jacket pockets in search of his lighter.

"The cemetery has its own raw beauty, you know, whatever the season," Baxter said. "No-one really knows how many bodies are in there. The official records disappeared decades ago. But even they wouldn't tell the whole story anyway. The earth out there is full of nameless dead, the deformed and the mad and the abandoned, their graves unmarked so their shame couldn't be traced back to their families. Accidents and suicides, some of them probably even genuine. Men . . . women . . . children who never tasted life beyond the womb."

Wren tensed at that, feeling something boil inside him. He was pretty sure Baxter realised what he'd said, a throwaway comment like a blade in his chest, but what the hell was he talking about, him and Nikki or—

"It isn't all bones and dust out there though, is it?" he said. "The ones who disappear, the ones like Vince. That's where they end up." Wren had meant it to sound like a question, but said aloud it didn't sound that way to him at all. It sounded like a challenge, an accusation. In defiance of the cold, he had started to sweat.

Slowly, Baxter turned to look at him and as he did so, a shaft of moonlight pierced the dirty window and imprinted the shadow of the mesh onto his face. Suddenly Baxter's blunt features were all angles, divided into a dozen segments like some strange, surrealist jigsaw. Only his eyes were missing pieces.

"Inspired, isn't it?" The jigsaw gained a smile. "Someone disappears and the last place anyone looks for a body is in a graveyard. Now, please, Harry."

Wren whipped his head to the right, saw Markham spitting out his cigarette unlit. Markham's hand was already emerging from his jacket, enfolding not his lighter but his gun.

Markham was fast but Wren was faster. He snatched his own handgun from his belt and brought it up. At the edge of his vision he could see that Baxter was moving too, a weapon in hand. But he was already killing Markham, squeezing the trigger, a nice controlled shot that would shear through Harry's breastbone like—

Click.

Wren had a second to look at the gun—the damned *empty* gun that Markham had given him—and then Baxter was there, his weapon raised like a club. Wren brought his arm up to shield his face as the gun descended, the butt slamming sharply into the back of his hand. His knuckles seemed to pop, radiating spokes of pain in both directions, down to his wrist and up to his fingertips. His fingers splayed, and the gun flew from his hand to spin off into a dark corner.

He opened his mouth to cry out, more in shock than anything else—the pain, though bad, seemed bearable, at this stage at least. But his yell remained unvoiced. Baxter was bringing the gun up now, and it slammed into the side of Wren's face with a cold, blinding weight. He reeled, his feet tangling, and Baxter's hard, flat-handed shove to his chest sent him sprawling. Wren tried to stand, but a solid kick in the ribs from Markham kept him down. He lay there, his chest full of spikes, his sight electric with hundreds of little white lights.

Unhurriedly, Baxter crossed to where he lay and knelt beside him, that icy shark's grin resurfacing.

"You'll have plenty of time to learn to appreciate Alderville's charms, Wren." He flipped the gun over in his hand, gripping it around the barrel, the butt jutting menacingly from his fist. He stood over Wren, and raised the weapon high.

"The rest of your life, in fact."
The gun swept down.

CHAPTER THREE

Four weeks ago . . .

IN THE LAST five or ten minutes or so, Wren had seen the girl he was here to hurt pass by her window a dozen times, back and forth, a swift-moving silhouette behind the half-open blinds. She hadn't paused to glance between them, and so Wren could presume that she hadn't seen the car in which he and McKenzie waited, parked quietly on the opposite side of the street to the girl's second-floor flat.

It was around nine in the evening, the end of November. A light, cold rain was falling, and though it wasn't much warmer inside the car, Wren could feel his shirt sticking wetly to the middle of his back.

"You okay, there?" McKenzie asked him. "You're sweating."

Wren thumbed a bead of perspiration from his eyebrow. His temples pounded. "I'm fine," he said. "A bit keyed up, that's all. I've never had to . . . " He shook his head. "I've never roughed up a woman before."

McKenzie nodded, and for a second Wren thought the other man actually understood his concerns, until McKenzie smiled.

"They bleed just like a bloke," he said. "It won't be a problem once you're up there. Just remember what Harry said. Don't touch her face, but anything below the neck is fair game."

Yes, Markham had *said that*, Wren thought. His guts had twisted as unpleasantly then as they were twisting now. He and McKenzie hadn't talked about why Baxter wanted the girl damaged. It was the Unwritten Rule. Wren guessed that

McKenzie had received the same message that he had, when Markham had called him an hour ago to relay Baxter's instructions. *She's got something on him,* Markham had said, the hint of a smile in his voice. *Incriminating snapshots. That's all you need to know.*

"Why the fuck isn't Baxter taking care of this himself?" Wren asked. The question had been bothering him since Markham's call. "I would have thought that if she was that much of a problem then he would have taken her to his precious Alderville."

McKenzie gave a little shrug. "You know how Baxter is," he said. "Nothing happens at Alderville unless he's there to enjoy it. He needs the girl fixed tonight, though, and apparently he's got a prior engagement he can't get out of. Someone's put the frighteners on him."

"The frighteners?" Wren couldn't imagine any "Prior Engagement" that Adam Baxter couldn't bribe, blackmail or murder his way out of, and he certainly couldn't conceive of anyone scaring him into doing something he didn't want to.

McKenzie laughed. "It's his Wedding Anniversary," he said. "She Who Must Be Obeyed gave him his orders weeks ago. They're in some fancy restaurant, somewhere." He glanced at his watch. "Should be tucking into their main courses just about now."

Wren thought of Adam Baxter, suited and booted, eating sirloin and sipping fine wine while someplace else a girl was to be hurt in his name. He imagined him, praising the meal and trying to keep the fearsome Mrs Baxter happy, and all the while he was yearning for his derelict asylum and to hear screams echoing within its walls. The thought of Baxter suffering like that amused and appalled Wren in equal measure. That bastard. Let him choke on his fucking steak.

McKenzie looked at his watch a moment longer, then tugged his sleeve forward to cover the dial. "We should probably get this done and dusted," he said. "Maybe get a pint and a chaser on the way home."

"Maybe." Wren nodded, though he had no intention of having a drink with Zach McKenzie, tonight or any other night. He tugged on his gloves. "Ten minutes."

Wren opened the passenger door and got out, repressing a shiver as the cold air hit his damp shirt. He hurried across the street, looking out for witnesses, but there was no-one around to see him busy himself at the door to the flats, picking the lock with ease even though his hands were shaking. Inside, he took the stairs to the second floor lightly, quietly, pausing at her door.

He listened. No muffled voices or music, no TV or radio to mask his intrusion. He would have to be careful. Markham had sketched the layout of the flat in his mind; beyond this door, there was a hallway with a bedroom on one side and a bathroom on the other, with the living room and the kitchen at the far end.

He picked the lock and eased the door inward as quietly as he could. If she was in the hallway or coming out of one of the rooms that adjoined it he would have to act fast. But the hallway was empty and as he closed the door behind him he caught a glimpse of her, hurrying past the open doorway to the living room. She was slim, maybe five-five, fair-haired. She didn't see him.

The first door he came to led to the bedroom and he glanced inside. The room was modestly furnished in differing shades of purple, and an open suitcase lay on the unmade bed, half-filled with unfolded, thrown-in clothes. She hadn't finished packing, would be back to this room any second now. This was where he would wait for her.

He stepped inside, noting the small collection of objects scattered on the bedside table. A set of keys, some coins, a couple of notes—and a square, crumpled slip of paper, about the size of a postcard. Something about the paper tugged at his memory, and he picked it up.

In the past he'd never been able to make them out, those blurred, radar-like pictures offered by proud parents, never been able to tell an arm from a leg in the monochrome fog. At least, not until that day he'd gone with Nikki to the hospital, and they had left with a picture of their own. After that, his perception had evolved, like the moment the eye unlocks the secret code of an optical illusion, and as he looked at the grainy image in his hand now he could see everything, the tiny, loose fist, the curve of a skull, the bud of a nose.

Incriminating snapshots, he heard Markham say again, and with it McKenzie's little reminder. *Anything below the neck is fair game.*

"You bastard," he whispered, Adam Baxter's face rising behind his simmering eyes. "You sick, sick bastard."

The photo trembled in his hand. Suddenly his entire body felt too heavy, as if every channel and cavity within him was flooded with wet cement, and for one awful moment, he feared he might pass out.

He didn't though. He managed to keep it together, though it seemed like his eyes had started to boil. Gently, he placed the picture back on to the table, surprised to note that his hand had steadied, staying on the photo a moment longer than it needed to, his fingertips resting on the little one's heart.

He heard footsteps, fast, behind him. The girl, hurrying along the hallway.

He scooped up the bunch of keys from the bedside table and moved to stand beside the doorway. As she entered he stepped forward, hooking an arm around her waist and pulling her to him. He only had a moment to make this work, to act in the seconds when she would be paralysed with shock.

"I've got a knife," he whispered.

She froze, and he placed the tip of a key just beneath her chin, not enough pressure to break the skin, but enough that she could feel what, to her, would seem like a sharp, deadly point.

"You need to listen to me," he said quietly, his lips almost touching her ear. "I don't want to hurt you. I'm not going to move the knife, but if you open your mouth to scream or if you try to run, the blade's gonna slice right up into your mouth. Raise your hand if you understand, but remember . . . " He closed his eyes for a moment. "Don't nod."

Slowly, she raised her right hand to shoulder height. It trembled. The back of it was inked, he saw, a fine, delicate butterfly between the knuckles of her thumb and forefinger. Her other hand never left her belly.

"Good. You can put it down again now."

As her hand began to lower, he went on, "Like I said, I don't want to hurt you, but that's what I've been sent here to do." Her body, already tensed, stiffened against him, but Wren kept his voice low and even. He felt sick.

"The man I work for . . . you know who he is. He thinks you're gonna make trouble for him. I don't think that. I think you're just gonna run. Have I got that right? Raise your hand for yes."

Her pale, shaking hand rose again, briefly, the butterfly taking flight, then dropped to her side once more, ready for another response.

"Okay," Wren said. "You want to run, and I don't want to hurt you. That seems like a good deal to me. I think what should happen here is that I take the knife away, and you just finish your packing and go. Do we have a deal?"

Her hand was up a moment before he finished the question.

He moved the key from beneath her throat, raising his hand to her eye-level and showing her what he held. She deflated, her shoulders sagging, her head lolling forward; if his arm hadn't still been looped around her waist, he thought she might have dropped to the carpet. The breath shuddered in and out of her.

He moved his arm and she took a few steps away from him, taking the keys from his hand as she did so. She went to the bed and sat down, returning the keys to the table, and picking up her ultrasound picture instead. She sat with it her lap, trembling.

"Are you okay?" he asked her.

She nodded. A tear dripped from her face and landed on the photo, and gently she brushed it away.

"You can't take him down," Wren told her. "If you think the kid gives you some kind of hold over him then—"

"I wasn't out to blackmail him or anything," she said suddenly. She looked up at him, her green eyes ringed with red. "I just wanted help . . . money for the baby. I wasn't going to tell anyone."

Wren nodded slowly. "You need to get away from here, and fast." He glanced at his watch. "Twenty minutes."

He started for the hallway. He was opening the front door when he heard her emerging from the bedroom behind him.

"Why, though?" she asked him. "Why didn't you . . . why didn't you do what you came here to do?"

Wren didn't turn around. "Twenty minutes," he said again, and left.

"How did it go?" McKenzie asked as soon as he was back in the car.

"It was fine," Wren answered tonelessly. He peeled off his gloves and stared at his hands.

"Great," McKenzie said. He reached into his jacket. "I'll call Markham, let him know we're all good here."

"No," Wren told him. His fingers were tangled loosely together, his hands pale, and in the dark interior of the car they looked small to him, embryonic. He clenched his fists. "Tell him later. We should go."

McKenzie hesitated for a moment, considering, then shrugged and started the engine. "So . . . " he said. "You still up for that pint?"

Wren shook his head. "Just drop me off home. I should probably check in on Nikki."

For a moment he thought that McKenzie might be about to make one of his trademark smart comments, but he just nodded and pulled out of their parking space. Wren was glad they weren't going to the pub. He was pretty sure he would be having a drink as soon as he got home, though. More than one.

They drove away. Wren stared at his fists with eyes that felt like undercooked meat.

Now . . .

McKenzie tugged the silver hipflask from his overcoat pocket, spun the cap, and downed a couple of swallows. The brandy burned in his throat and blossomed pleasantly in his chest. They were waiting in a cramped, filthy office just off the main entrance hall. Before he left, Markham had set up a couple of small electric lanterns around the room, and now McKenzie was leaning against one of the office's two adjacent filing cabinets, watching Vince's shadow sweep back and forth across the tiled wall as the other man paced the little room, trying to keep warm.

Abruptly Vince stopped as he noted the flask. "What the fuck's that?" he asked sharply. He held out his hand to McKenzie. "Scotch? Brandy? Hand it over."

"Sorry, Vince." McKenzie gave the hipflask a little shake, listening to at least another couple of shots of liquor splashing around inside, though he doubted Vince would be able to hear it above the chattering of his teeth. "Sounds to me like the well is dry." He tucked the flask back into his overcoat. "I would have brought more if I'd thought you wanted some."

"I don't fucking want it," Vince told him. "I fucking need it. I'm gonna get hyperthermia at this rate." He hugged himself and began rubbing furiously at his scrawny biceps to generate some heat. "This is meant to be all planned out. It's a fucking shambles."

McKenzie laughed. "What's with the attitude all of a sudden?" he asked. "You turning into a proper diva now you've moved into acting?"

"This isn't acting," Vince snapped back. "I'm bloody freezing to death. Where the fuck's Markham?"

"Right here, Vincent." Markham entered the office, carrying a black plastic refuse bag. He set it down on the desk. "Happy Christmas."

"About bloody time," Vince said. "I can't feel my face."

"Just be grateful you can't see it," Markham smiled. "You look like death warmed over."

"I'm not even that fucking warm," Vince muttered sourly, opening the bag and tugging out a tangle of clothes.

Markham turned to McKenzie. "Did you give him the brandy?"

"Oops," McKenzie said. "I must have forgot. Sorry." He reached into his pocket and pulled out the hipflask.

Scowling, Vince reached for it—but Markham intercepted it, plucking the flask from McKenzie's hand. He unscrewed the top and took a shot.

"Sorry, Vince." He smiled. "Privileges of rank."

"Bastards, the pair of you." Vince scowled, and returned to the bag. The first item he pulled out was a dark grey hooded jacket; he dragged it on as quickly as he could, zipping it up to his throat, then reached into the bag again to see what else he could find.

"You should have let me put on a coat before we left," he said. "It's fucking winter, for Christ's sake."

Markham shrugged. "You were meant to act as though we'd taken you by surprise. It would have looked a bit suspicious if you'd been sitting there waiting for us in a fucking scarf and mittens."

"You were early though," Vince had found a pair of fingerless gloves in the tangle of clothes and was tugging them on to his shaking hands. "You could have at least given me time to put my shoes on."

Markham nodded. "I thought of that." He pulled his hand out from behind his back and offered Vince a pair of tattered sneakers. They looked like they might have been a crisp white when new, but now they were the colour of a cigar-stained ceiling, the laces threaded with mould. "We don't want you wearing a hole in your socks."

Vince took the shoes, inspecting them warily. "What the fuck are these? They're not mine."

Markham took another sip of brandy. "The previous owner won't be needing them."

"Previous . . . " Vince's eyebrows arched as understanding dawned. "Oh, for fuck's sake, Markham . . . dead man's shoes?"

Markham shrugged, gesturing at the black plastic bag on the table. "Dead man's everything," he said. "Look, Vince, I don't give a fuck whether you wear any of this stuff or not, just make your fucking mind up. Baxter's already gone to get the girl so he's gonna want to get this underway as soon as possible."

"What?" Vince sounded alarmed. "So Wren's on his own? What if he gets loose?"

"Relax," Markham said. "He's down in the cellar, trussed up good and tight. Baxter wants—" Suddenly his phone chirped, an incoming message. He slipped it from his pocket and squinted at the display. "Talk of the devil . . . " he murmured, then looked up at the other two men, his features hard.

"It's Baxter," he said. "He's ready."

CHAPTER FOUR

AWAKENING FELT LIKE rising to the top of some churning, murky lake. Wren felt the weight of it, trying to drag him back down, but there was light beyond the surface, and he forced himself toward it.

He kept thinking about the first time he'd seen Nikki, a pretty girl on a train, reading a paperback. She'd used a playing card as a bookmark back then, an ace of hearts, and he'd sat two seats away fascinated by the way she tapped the frayed edge of the card against her lips while she was reading. He was no romantic, and he would never concede even to himself that there was such a thing as love at first sight, but there had been something about that girl that captured him, made him think of her as a piece he hadn't even realised he was missing.

As he rose, there seemed to be shapes in the water. Doorways, stairs. Torch beams, crossing in the dark. Voices, too, muffled by that underwater feeling, but familiar. He heard McKenzie laughing. Wren's shins burned, skinned against stone as they dragged him.

He had no concept of how long it was until he reached the surface. Minutes. Hours. It felt like forever.

He opened his eyes, blinking. A grey room, bare walls. He could just about make out an open door in front of him and a corridor beyond, but the room was mostly a blur of light and shade.

He was sitting, a hard, wooden chair. His wrists were cuffed behind him. His skull throbbed where Baxter's gun had struck, the scalp bunched into a hard knot crusted with dried blood. He'd been stripped of his jacket and it felt like the sleeves of his shirt had been rolled up almost to his elbows—the skin of his forearms was spiny with gooseflesh.

Carefully, he began to draw his hands apart, biting back a yell as yet more agony chewed at his shoulder muscles; his arms had been immobile for what might have been hours, the sockets feeling filled with broken glass. He parted his hands as far as they would go, until the cuffs dug sharply into his wrists, realizing that the chain between them was looped somehow through the back of the chair.

He let his arms go limp. *Fuck.*

After a moment, two blurred points of light resolved themselves into small electric lanterns in the corners of the room, and a shadow sharpened to Adam Baxter, standing with his back to Wren, his hand pressed lightly against the bare wall.

Wren leaned back in the chair, making at it creak, and Baxter spared him a glance before returning his attention to the wall. He began to run his gloved fingertip along one of the many cracks spider-webbing the plaster.

"Welcome back to the land of the living, Wren," he said quietly. "For now, anyway."

"Baxter." The words rasped out of his throat like sandpaper. "What . . . what the fuck's going on?"

Baxter didn't turn around. "You're still in Alderville, in the cellar. It might not look like much now but believe me, if these walls could talk . . . " His finger traced the spider web. "But Alderville's a place for secrets. It always has been."

"Why . . . " Wren licked his arid lips. "Why are you doing this?"

Baxter turned. He held up his hand for silence, and Wren, his vision sharpening, saw that the gloved palm and fingertips were pale with plaster dust.

"The man in charge here was a Dr Von Fleisher," Baxter told him. "The name translates loosely into English as 'Noble Butcher.' Interesting, yes?"

Without waiting for a reply, he went on. "He was a visionary, in his way. He had this theory that a person could access certain . . . places, if the brain was reconfigured correctly. Astral planes, other dimensions, the Twilight Zone, whatever." He walked forward, gesturing at the dank walls of the cellar. "Down here was where he did all the surgery, all the experiments. Of course, when word got out what he was doing he was mocked, persecuted, driven to suicide. People forgot the Noble part of his name and just called him the Butcher."

Baxter shook his head, sighing. "Society's like that, though, isn't it? Always judging things it doesn't understand. Take me, for example. In society's eyes I'm a criminal, a murderer. But I'm just a businessman, Wren, albeit an unorthodox one, and like any employer I just want the best person for the job."

He moved to stand in front of Wren. "I knew you were losing your nerve. I could smell it on you. I don't know if was the thought of your impending fatherhood that made you soft, or if it was when your fatherhood was no longer . . . impending." He smiled. "But when Caitlin came along with her little snapshot, well, I knew I'd found the perfect opportunity to test your loyalty."

Wren frowned up at him—*Caitlin?*—then he realised. The incriminating snapshot. The girl with the butterfly tattoo.

"Ordinarily I'd have paid her off and given her a kick up the arse as a bon voyage, but when you weakened, when you let her go . . . " He shrugged. "I had to take more drastic measures. Fortunately, Markham was up to the job even if you weren't."

Wren lowered his head. He'd tried to do the right thing, tried to save *someone* . . . all for nothing. His mouth tasted like it was full of burnt paper. When he raised his head again, Baxter was behind him.

"You should consider this the termination of your employment, Wren, amongst other things. But I'm not a monster. I know that Christmas is a time to spend with your loved ones. That's why I've arranged it so you won't be facing this ordeal alone."

He placed his gloved hands on Wren's shoulders. Wren struggled, repulsed, but the cuffs were still in place and Baxter's grip too strong. He could see torchlight in the corridor, see Markham bringing another person into the cellar.

He heard the smile in Baxter's voice. "I promised I'd have you back with her by midnight."

"I promised I'd have you back with her by midnight," she heard Baxter say as Markham pushed her into the room, his hand clamped tightly to her arm.

Nikki thought that the hours since she had opened the door to Adam Baxter had been some of the most confusing and frightening of her life. She'd been surprised to see him, of course, on Christmas Eve of all times, and she remembered thinking that he must have bad news for her about Paul, that being the wife of a criminal was the like being a cop's wife, in that each of them dreaded a knock at the door from their man's colleagues. She had no real liking for Baxter but was glad of his smile when she invited him in, asked him if everything was okay.

As it turned out, everything was pretty fucking *far* from okay.

They'd burst through the door, Baxter and the other one, McKenzie. She'd ran through the house, knowing she wouldn't have time for a phone call but heading for the kitchen, where the knives where. They got to her before she reached it. She managed a kick between McKenzie's legs that left him gasping, but Baxter had caught her with a hard, sweeping slap, knocking her to the carpet.

They had brought tape for her mouth and rope for her hands and feet. There was a long journey in a car, her body trussed up uncomfortably on the back seat. The roads had gotten more uneven when they left the motorway, and even before they stopped and lifted her out of the car she had known where they were headed.

Alderville.

Paul had talked about it only once, said it was somewhere Baxter conducted business. He said that Baxter liked it out there because it was remote and there was no chance of *business* being disturbed. He'd said no more about it, and Nikki had been unable to make herself ask. She had been afraid that if she had, the horrifying possibility would exist that she might begin to love her husband a little less.

They'd taken her to a room on the second floor, some kind of ward or dormitory. The room was long and wide, large enough to hold about a dozen old-style metal hospital beds, though she could see now that only five remained, two on one side of the room, three on the other. Only one of them still had its mattress, but all of them still had those leather restraining straps swinging from the frames. The room's lone window was at the far end of the room, its pane filthy behind a sheet of metallic mesh.

McKenzie had used one of the leather straps to secure her to the rusting wreckage of one of the beds. Both men had stayed with her for a little while, talking only when they were in the corridor, in hushed tones. They had departed only when she heard another car pull up outside.

She had no idea how long they had left her there, and her mind had filled with the most terrible thoughts . . . rape, murder . . . She had sat on that filthy floor listening to the muffled voices downstairs and sobbed, just wanting Paul here, needing him here *now*.

Eventually, Baxter had returned, untied her, and taken her back down to the entrance hall. McKenzie and Harry Markham were there along with another man she didn't recognise. She'd been left with Markham for maybe ten minutes, until he had brought her down here, to the cellars.

As soon as she saw her husband she struggled, wanting

only to run to him, but Markham twisted her arm savagely behind her back, keeping her close. He drew his gun and jabbed it into her ribs.

"Settle the fuck down," he hissed. "Unless you want the pair of you dead a lot sooner."

She kept thrashing in his grip, feeling something tear in her strained shoulder and dismissing it, reaching up with her free hand to claw at Markham's face.

"Fuck it!" Markham spat. "Tell this bitch to calm down, Wren, or I'll blow out her kidneys in front of you! Tell her!"

"Nikki!" Wren cried, and something in his voice, so hoarse and broken, slowed her down. "Not now, love, please! Just cool it!"

She managed to still herself, though she couldn't stop trembling, couldn't keep from crying. "Paul, what is this? What the fuck's happening?"

"It's okay," he told her. He was keeping his gaze level but his voice shook. "We're gonna be okay."

"Come on, now, Wren," Baxter said behind him. "It's unkind to lie to her."

"Baxter," he said hoarsely. "This has got nothing to do with her. I was the one who fucked up." He licked his lips. "Baxter, please . . . "

Baxter's hands squeezed his shoulders. "She's here because you're going to die tonight. My wish is to cause you as much pain as possible between that point and this. Physical pain is all well and good, but I've been doing this a long time, and I'm pretty sure you'll expire from your injuries before I'm even close to satisfied. But if I throw in a little emotional pain before you go . . . well, maybe then I can go to sleep happy tonight. You're going to suffer, Wren, and Nicola here gets to watch."

Paul shook his head. He stared at her. *I'm sorry,* he mouthed.

"We should get started." Baxter turned to a small trestle table behind him. "I'm giving a reading at Mass later." He nodded at Nikki. "Hold her. If she tries to break loose again, shoot her in the guts."

He held up the object he'd picked up from the table, something squat and metallic, with a short, copper-coloured nozzle jutting from the top. It was only when he adjusted a small valve on the side of the nozzle, only when the sour sting of gas hissed into the room, that Nikki's mind allowed her to recognise the object for what it was.

A blowtorch.

Baxter pulled a lighter from his pocket. He held it close to the nozzle and placed his thumb on the ignition wheel, then hesitated, a smile cutting across his features.

"And if *he* screams," Baxter said to Markham. "Shoot her in the head."

Markham moved the gun from her ribs to her temple, as if to confirm to Baxter that he understood. Baxter nodded approvingly, and slid his thumb over the wheel. The blowtorch's yellow flame bloomed, tiny sparks diving in and out of its shifting edge. Baxter made a small adjustment to the valve, and the flame narrowed to a thin beam, startlingly blue in the dim room. He leaned forward, his hands moving to behind the chair, where Nikki couldn't see them. Somehow, that was worse.

There was a soft, crackling sound, and Paul stiffened in the chair, his lips pressed together in a hard, white line. Sweat blossomed at his temples.

His eyes were wide, fixed on hers. He was focussing totally on her, she realised, on the gun at her temple, and using that focus to keep his scream inside, to keep her alive.

But when he struggled, still silent, when the scent of crisping hair became a thicker, greasier smell, Nikki found herself crying out *for* him, a long, screeching song from her heart outwards.

Baxter paused. He frowned briefly at her screaming like a librarian irritated by a loud sneeze, then leaned forward with the lighter again.

The room filled with the smell of summer barbeques.

I'm gonna be sick, Vince thought.

It was a real possibility. He felt like he had a belly full of snakes, twisting and writhing, churning whatever was left of the ham sandwich he'd had while he was waiting for Markham and Wren—thrashing, burning Wren—to arrive.

He stood with McKenzie in the corridor outside the cellar. He'd taken a few steps away from the open door as soon as he realised what Baxter was about to do, but McKenzie was still watching, his eyes bright, his aggravating little smirk present and correct. Sick fucker.

Vince rubbed a hand across his eyes. The bile burned in his throat. Maybe if he got some air . . .

"I'm going outside for a piss," he told McKenzie. "I feel like I've got fucking icebergs in my bladder."

"What?" McKenzie looked unconvinced, he thought. "You're gonna miss all the good stuff."

Vince shrugged. "I've seen it all before," he said casually. His stomach boiled.

McKenzie's brows drew together. "Baxter won't like you leaving."

"He'll like it a lot less if I piss all over the floor. I'll be ten minutes."

"You know what I think." McKenzie's smirk broadened. "I think you're wimping out. You look like you're about to chuck your guts up. All getting a bit much for you, is it?"

"Fuck you," Vince said. "I'll be as quick as I can."

He walked away, knowing that McKenzie was watching him and so he kept his pace as even as possible until he was out of sight. Even then, once he started hurrying, he knew he couldn't outrun the screams.

Vince never made it outside. He got as far as a corridor on the first floor before he puked. Afterward, he stood with his hands planted on his thighs, breathing hard. His eyes streamed and his sinuses stung, flushed with bile. It was no picnic, but he welcomed it over the stink of Wren's burning flesh.

Jesus. *Jesus.* He'd known that Baxter was planning to make Wren suffer, that was fine with him, but he'd expected the pliers or a razor, not the flame.

That *smell* . . . it had made him feel ten again, made him remember the night his Dad had taken him to the firework display in Shelby Park. Instead of launching skyward, one of the rockets had veered into the crowd and hit a kid standing no more than a few feet away from him. It had been November, and the little girl had her hood pulled up against the cold. The rocket had flown right into it. He supposed the crowd must have screamed, though he didn't remember it. He didn't think the girl had time. But the smell, the acrid stink of burning hair and scorched flesh as everything inside the hood burst into flames, that had stayed with him. Even now, the smoky breath of beef on a grill repulsed him. But the girl, and now Wren, the stench of scorched living flesh. It was worse, a thick, greasy fog that somehow . . . *squirmed* in his nose and mouth.

For a minute he thought he would puke again, but when the feeling passed he straightened, wiping his mouth with his sleeve. He spat. He couldn't go back, not yet, but when he did he knew he'd be asking McKenzie for his hipflask. He would—

A sound like a heavy footfall onto thin ice came from behind him.

Vince turned, taking a step back, almost into his own vomit. There was a thin, horizontal fracture across the wall on the other side of the corridor, and as he watched the split lengthened, began to widen. Slices of plaster fell, exposing slats of rotten wood. It sounded like there was something behind the wall, something slithering, and Vince considered the unpleasant probability that the spaces behind Alderville's walls would be crawling with rats.

"Big fucking rats, if they are," he murmured, as the crack

opened a little wider. Warily, he approached the wall, thinking that yes, the sound might be their wiry, vermin bodies sliding over each other, but surely he should be hearing more, their squeaks or the scrape of their claws. *Something.* But there was only that slithering hiss, rising as he reached the wall.

More plaster tumbled, and between the slats he could see the darkness beyond. He wished he'd thought to bring a torch. He peered into the blackness and thought he could see . . . movement. He told himself that it could be rats. The movement in the dark looked like it was composed of lots of shapes rather than one, shifting, entwining, shuddering, that hiss almost seeming to come from within the mound.

Suddenly the hiss stopped, and Vince had the strangest impression that his presence had been noticed.

The bulk behind the wall approached him, a kind of pulsating, rolling motion. He could hear it sliding over the floor. There was a smell now, too. Meat, but not the odour of charred flesh this time. This was a heavy, sickening cloud of tissue dissolving, skin peeling from muscle, offal on a hot day, squeezing between the slats to engulf him. He gagged, taking a step back, but the thing was already pressing at the slats now, grey, wiry tendrils snaking out between the wood. He thought he could see some kind of opening in the mass, a lipless mouth filled with a collision of mismatched teeth.

The tendrils reached out to him.

Vince screamed.

CHAPTER FIVE

MCKENZIE, STANDING IN the corridor outside the cellar, thought that he was the only one who heard it, until he glanced in at Markham and saw the older man frown, and turn his gaze to the ceiling. He could see that Markham was thinking the same thing that he had, that the high, spiralling shriek somewhere above them might be in his imagination, a mental echo of the woman's screams.

She'd shut the fuck up now, at least. Christ, she had a set of lungs on her, but a minute or two ago her screams had dwindled to a run of croaky, hitching sobs as she watched Baxter work, her eyes huge. She had heard the other scream too, though, judging by the way her eyes had flicked upwards.

McKenzie was pretty sure that Baxter hadn't heard it, though whether that was because of the roar of the blowtorch or simply because he was so engrossed in his work, McKenzie couldn't say. And as for Wren . . . Wren's head lolled forward, and though he was still twitching as the flame scorched his hand, McKenzie guessed that he'd finally blacked out.

Markham had heard it, though. The two men exchanged a glance, and it was Markham who finally called out to Baxter. His call was ignored, so he called out again.

Baxter looked up from his work, scowling. "What?"

Markham hesitated before replying. "We heard a shout. From upstairs."

No, we didn't, McKenzie thought. *We heard a scream.*

"A shout?" Baxter stepped away from Wren, extinguishing the blowtorch.

McKenzie spoke from the doorway. "Vince went up there

a few minutes ago. He needed a slash." Noting Baxter's look of disapproval he quickly went on. "Do you want me to check it out?"

Baxter returned the blowtorch to the table. "No," he said. "We both will. Vince should know better than to wander off during proceedings. He and I are going to have words. Besides . . . " He pressed his fists into the small of his back and stretched. "I could use a break."

"What about the girl?" Markham asked. "You want me to cuff her and come with you?"

Baxter considered. "You stay here," he said. "Keep an eye on Wren. But we'll take her with us. If he wakes up, play a few mind games with him. Tell him I've decided to give her a tour of the cemetery."

"Why are you doing this to us?" the woman asked him suddenly, twisting in Markham's grip. Her voice was pleasingly hoarse from all her screaming and that, combined with the way the tears had streaked the make-up around her eyes, gave her a certain sexiness that McKenzie approved of. "What's fucking wrong with you?"

Baxter didn't answer her. Some of her spittle had landed on his overcoat, and he casually brushed at his lapel with his gloved hand. He turned to McKenzie.

"You take her," he said. "She can keep us company while we investigate this . . . " He smiled. "*Shout* that's got you and Markham so spooked."

A scream, McKenzie thought. His eyes met Markham's and he knew that however carefully the other man had chosen his words, he knew exactly what they had heard. *We heard a fucking scream.*

Ten minutes later. . .

"Looks like I was right," McKenzie said, grimacing. He pointed his torch at the greasy pool on the floor. "Vincey *was* ready to chuck his guts up."

They were standing in a corridor on the first floor. McKenzie's hand was folded tightly around Nikki's wrist. Baxter was a few feet away, playing his torchlight across a hole in the wall on the other side of the corridor.

He didn't even seem like he needed the torch, Nikki thought. Whereas McKenzie had carefully picked his way through Alderville's corridors, mindful of debris and obstructions, Baxter had stormed ahead, negotiating stairs and passageways seemingly without hesitation, as though he knew the place inside out. Often his torch hadn't even been pointed in the direction in which they were headed.

He seemed to need it now, though, and something of the quizzical tilt of his head made Nikki realise why. He really did know Alderville like the back of his hand, every inch of it, and the reason he was frowning now as he cast his torchlight over the wall, tracing the edges of the fractured plaster and wood, was because the hole in the wall was something new, unexpected.

"Come here," he said.

McKenzie tugged at her wrist and moved to join him. "What is it?"

"This," Baxter said, sweeping his torch beam into the blackness. Nikki squinted, but there was nothing to see. Some debris. A few patches of what looked like stagnant water. Blackness.

McKenzie shrugged. "It's a hole. Big wow. The place is falling apart."

"It wasn't here earlier this evening," Baxter told him. His eyebrow twitched. "Holes just don't make themselves, do they?"

"What are you saying?" McKenzie asked. "You think it looks like something came out of the wall?"

"No." Baxter shone his torch into the maw, swept its light over the plaster and stone on the other side of the hole, the broken slats of rotten wood that jutted not into the corridor, but into the cavity beyond. "I think it looks like something was pulled *into* it."

He reached for his phone.

"But first, the forecast for tonight . . . "

Wren blinked, or thought he did. Markham had gone out into the corridor, leaving him alone, but that was okay. A television set had appeared in the corner of the room, a big old square affair, state of the art in the nineteen-eighties, but prehistoric-looking now. Wren was sure that it hadn't been there earlier—well, almost sure, there seemed to be a little static in his attic at the moment—but its presence, sudden or otherwise, didn't seem to bother him.

He stared at the images flickering on the screen, or thought he did. A familiar man in a grey suit was smiling out at him, and Wren felt an absurd surge of gratitude at the sight of a friendly face, even if it was just the weatherman. He was speaking, his voice soft and reassuring, gesturing at the floating graphic behind him. Wren frowned. This couldn't be right. The graphic was indeed dotted with little symbols—a cloud here, a sweep of arrows there—but it definitely wasn't the satellite snapshot of the British Isles that he might expect. It was his own naked body, battered and bruised, adrift in some strange black void.

"Well, it's a grim outlook for the next few hours," the weatherman told him, his smile unchanging. "With severe damage starting here and spreading." He pointed behind him at the blistered wreck of Wren's hand. Little dark clouds appeared around it, lightning aglow in their depths, and in the real world, the scorching, *exposed* sensation of his injury clicked up a couple of notches.

The weatherman went on, "We can expect numerous outbreaks of homicidal behaviour throughout the night, so take care if you're planning to escape. Storm clouds are gathering, and I'm afraid it's going to be rather an unhappy close to Christmas Eve, most likely ending in a hail of bullets. Well, that's all for now, Wren. Goodnight, and—oh, excuse me."

His phone was ringing. He reached inside his jacket for it, flashing Wren an embarrassed smile, and lifted the mobile to his ear. "Yeah? What's happening?"

He listened for a moment, his expression darkening, and when he spoke again his voice was harsher, the legacy of a pack a day habit, and much more familiar.

"What do you mean, he's missing?"

Wren snapped back into consciousness. He blinked, for real this time, as the room gradually drifted back into focus. The television was gone, of course, and there was only the cellar, the grey, crumbling plaster.

His burnt hand radiated pain, infecting every nerve in his body with a pulsing, glassy ache. He was still in the chair, his wrists still cuffed.

Beyond the open door in front of him, he could see a torch beam, its edges sharpening. Markham's voice grew clearer as he returned along the corridor. "Nah, he's still spark out. He looks like shit, though. Not sure I'll be able to get him on his feet."

Markham was taking him somewhere, but where? Outside to kill him and lose him among the nameless dead in Alderville's graveyard? Wren didn't think so. *He's missing*, Markham had said, surprised, and so it seemed that something had gone awry with Baxter's scheme, an accident or something. Whatever was happening, if Markham was taking him anywhere, he'd have to unlock the cuffs.

Take care if you're planning to escape, the weatherman had said. Good advice. Wren looked at the doorway a moment more, his plan forming, then closed his eyes and let his head slump forward.

Markham entered the room, Baxter's muffled voice buzzing from his mobile like an angry wasp, and more than anything else Wren wished that his hands were free, free to throttle the bastard's last sour breath out of him, free to touch Nikki again and tell her how sorry he was—

"Okay, okay, I'll sort it," Markham was saying. "Just give

me a couple of minutes, okay? I . . . hello?" A pause, then a bleep as he hung up on the already-dead line. "Bastard."

Wren sensed him draw nearer, keys jingling as he fished them from his pocket.

"Fucking carry him, then," Markham snarled, twisting his voice into a crude mimic of Baxter's tones. "What does he think I am, a fucking pack horse? Bollocks."

The footsteps stopped, and Wren opened his eyes a little, his chin still resting on his chest. Markham was right in front of him now. He saw the other man's shoes, brown leather, frosted with plaster dust. The lace of the right was coming undone slightly and there was a dark smear on the tip of the left, a stain that looked like—

My blood, Wren realised. He closed his eyes, feeling something cold and murderous uncoil lazily in the pit of his stomach. It was a blind, almost reptilian instinct, seductive enough almost to eclipse the pain, and for that alone Wren welcomed it.

Markham moved behind him, and a second or two later Wren heard him set the torch down, felt him tugging at the cuffs. "Dunno why he's making such a song and dance about this, anyway," Markham muttered to himself sourly. "I remember back when he would have just put a bullet in your head and been done with it. But no, thanks to you, I'm out here in the middle of fucking nowhere, Christmas Eve, when I could be at home tucked up in bed, trying to fend off the wife after a couple of sherries."

He took hold of the cuff around Wren's wrist, the right one, and Wren heard the little key sliding into the lock—but it didn't turn.

Markham leaned close, his lips almost touching Wren's ear. "You know, Wren, maybe I owe you a pint."

Chuckling to himself, he removed the cuffs, and as Markham began to straighten Wren jabbed his elbow savagely back into the other man's face. The impact shot fresh bolts of agony the length of his arm, but it gave him the moment he needed to get to his feet.

He'd caught Markham square in the mouth, he saw. Markham stumbled back a little, dropping the keys, his bared teeth streaked with red. He was reaching for the handgun tucked into his belt.

Wren leapt at him. He lashed out, but his arms felt like lead, barely connected to his body, and Markham ducked the blow easily, slamming a punch into Wren's middle that shunted the breath from his lungs. For a heartbeat, Wren slumped against him like a tired boxer, until Markham pushed him away with a hard, flat-handed shove. He staggered back, knocking the chair aside, before his numbed legs tangled beneath him and he went sprawling.

After a moment he managed to sit up. Markham was glaring at him, his breath coming in harsh, wheezing gasps.

"Bastard," Markham spat. "I'll fucking kill you myself."

His hand dropped to the pistol at his belt—and found it missing. He looked down, his fingers seemingly welded to the place where the gun had been only seconds before. Then his hot, murderous gaze turned back to Wren, widening as he found the weapon suddenly in the hand of his captive.

"Stay back," Wren croaked, dismayed to hear no weight in his voice. Still, the weight in his hand proved persuasive enough. Markham not only halted, but took a step in retreat.

"Okay," Wren went on. "Where—"

But the question went unfinished—without warning, the floor between them blew upward as if a grenade had detonated beneath it, though there was no heat, no light or flames, just the screech of twisting metal and cracking stone, and the blizzard of fragments that slashed at Wren's face and the exposed skin of his hands.

He caught a glimpse of Markham, on the other side of the eruption, pitched off his feet and thrown back against the wall. His face was slack with shock. Markham's torch flew across the room, a blur of light, striking the wall somewhere behind Wren and clattering to the floor. And then something—some *thing*—was winding and twisting its way out of the floor in a surreal birth.

Wren squinted at it with burning eyes. He couldn't make out many details through the great cloud of dust and debris mushrooming out of the void in its wake, but its bulk, the snake-like way it moved, gave the impression of a writhing, sinewy strength.

The shape kept hurtled upward, and for a moment Wren thought that it would keep going, that its momentum would propel it straight through the roof like the glass elevator in that story he'd liked as a kid, but instead the thing hunched and curved its mass forward, almost a question mark, scraping against the ceiling rather than penetrating it.

Dead bulbs exploded. Plaster fell.

A stench was rising with it, a filthy gangrenous fog that soaked the air around Wren and made his stomach twist into tight, convulsive knots. On the other side of the dust cloud, he could hear Markham retching.

He struggled to stand. His right hand still gripped the gun and without thinking he tried to push himself from the floor with his left—his burnt flesh crackled agonisingly as soon as it touched the floor, as if he'd plunged his hand into a bucketful of salt, and he cried out.

The creature spun its bulk to face him, dislodging more of the ceiling and making what was left of the floor around it rumble ominously. It dipped toward him slightly and paused, almost as if it were studying him, though it had no features, no face at all that Wren could see. But now that it was still, caught in the flood of light from the torch somewhere behind him, he could make out more of its nightmare design than he would have liked.

The squirming grey hide was a map of corruption, like a thing skinned and left out in the sun to rot. Defleshed, decaying, and yet somehow hideously alive. Its bulk was threaded with gristly ropes of tendon; the ropes flexed and loosened, loosened and flexed, giving it movement as if they were puppeteer's strings. Scores of glossy black beetles navigated its inhuman contours, clustering in places like scabs on a wound, but that wasn't the worst of it. Now Wren could see the islands of what looked like spoiled meat scattered across its surface, and embedded in one of them, one that was almost level with Wren's face . . .

He knew what he was seeing, though reason—or as much reason as he might be capable of applying right now—told him it was impossible. And still the horror of it touched him like a cold kiss to the heart.

Locked within a tangle of frayed tissue was a human eye.

It was unmistakable, though the unblinking oval was stretched and distorted by the tidal shifting of the thing's hide. The iris had been bleached ivory, ringing a sightless pupil as black as a gunshot wound. A wrinkled scrap of lid remained, and this close, Wren could see how the long, dark lashes were clotted with soil.

Suddenly the thing reared away from him, and Wren saw that while his gaze had been locked with that terrible unseeing orb, Markham had been moving, his back pressed to the wall. Clearly the creature had sensed him trying to edge his way around it, and whipped around to block his path.

Wren took his chance. He pushed himself to his feet, remembering to favour his wounded hand this time, and made for the door.

"Wren!" Markham yelled.

Wren stopped and looked back. The thing had Markham trapped against the wall now. When he edged left, the creature swept forward to intercept him. A few abortive steps to his right and suddenly it was there too. In desperation, Markham picked up the chair from where it had fallen and held it front of him, thrusting it at the monstrosity like an old fashioned lion tamer, but the creature simply swung itself at him again and knocked the makeshift shield from his grasp. Markham shrank back against the wall, his eyes huge.

Wren turned away.

"Shoot it!" The voice was thin and wavering, almost a shriek and utterly unlike any sound Wren had thought Markham capable of making. He turned back.

"Shoot it!" Markham nearly-shrieked again, his face as grey as the plaster wall behind him. "Wren, you've got the gun, for fuck's sake, shoot it!"

Wren brought the pistol up. The thing seemed to sense his intent and reared away from Markham, looming high above them. Wren spared it a glance, took aim, and made his shot.

Markham's kneecap exploded.

He screamed, no nearly about it this time, and fell forward. What remained of his left leg folded beneath him at an angle that was impossibly, hideously wrong, taking the last of his kneecap with it. The lower half of his leg seemed to topple away from him, the sole of one of his dusty, bloodied shoes suddenly level with his waist.

Wren swung his aim around to the creature but it was already moving, swooping down toward Markham's screaming form. It smashed into him, and the scream became a fountain of blood.

The thing drew back and flexed, arching like a scorpion's tail, and for two panicked heartbeats Wren saw what it had done to Markham. It was a brief, terrible glimpse, but Wren's horror stretched the moment, imprinted it forever inside him.

The man's torso had been blown open by the impact, an inelegant autopsy venting steam into the freezing room. Markham was still alive though, and conscious, though whether or not he was cognizant Wren couldn't say. His eyes—startlingly blue in that white face—rolled glassily in their sockets, while his bloody mouth worked and twitched soundlessly.

Then the creature swooped forward again, and Markham was gone.

Something hit Wren, pressed into his back—the door frame—and he realised that his legs had been taking him backward of their own volition. He stumbled out into the corridor, casting a last look at the grisly tableau now framed in the doorway. The monster, terrible and looming. Harry Markham, whose wife was expecting him home in time for Christmas Dinner, was little more than a smear on the concrete floor—in the torchlight and shadows, his blood might have been some rich, dark wine.

Wren scooped up the torch from where it had fallen, holding it as best he could with his damaged hand, and reeled away from the scene, heading for the stairwell door at the end of the corridor. His legs were numb and unsteady as stilts, and the corridor itself seemed endless, the door impossibly distant. He stumbled, staggered, could barely walk.

But when he heard the gunshots, echoing somewhere above him, Wren found that he could run.

CHAPTER SIX

"**W**AIT," BAXTER SAID.

They paused at the door leading into the entrance hall. Standing a little behind Baxter, Nikki peered into the shadows. It was almost pitch-black in there; the heavily-meshed windows were too murky to admit much natural light, and even Baxter's torch beam, swept from left to right and back again, picked out little more than silhouettes. The main desk. An abandoned IV stand.

"What is it?" McKenzie hissed. Nikki felt his grip tighten painfully around her wrist.

"Not sure," Baxter replied after a moment. He swung the torchlight again, this time following its arc with the barrel of his handgun. "Thought I saw something."

McKenzie scanned the gloom. "I don't see anything."

"What's up, Adam?" Nikki asked him. "Scared of the dark?"

He turned and thrust his face into hers, and for one mad moment she thought he was going to kiss her. Suddenly she could smell his aftershave—something expensive, soured now by sweat.

"No." His tone was vicious. "I'm more worried that dead brat of yours is gonna jump out and shout *boo!*"

A sickening, unwelcome warmth blossomed in the middle of her chest and behind her eyes. She glanced across at McKenzie, but he was looking away from her, his lips thin and white like a scar.

"You bastard," she said softly. Baxter's breath and hers mingled in the chill air like waltzing ghosts. "You evil bastard."

He smiled at her coldly. "And don't you forget it." He nodded to McKenzie. "Let's go."

He took a step through the door, then paused to glare at Nikki. "And keep her close," he told McKenzie. "She's unfinished business."

They started moving. Nikki glared at Baxter's broad back. She wanted to kill him. The desire was very real, in a way that she had never thought herself capable of feeling, not even with that tangle of blind rage that had become her constant companion since they had lost Melissa. That rage, that cursing of the universe and its random injustices, that had kept her awake at night, had made even the slightest touch of Paul's hand toxic to her, had made her keep her naming of their baby—her baby—a secret. *Melissa.* Her Grandmother's name.

She thought of Paul now though, her Paulie, battered and broken and locked in the cellar, and suddenly wished she had told him.

"Hold it," McKenzie said urgently. "Back there."

Baxter swung the torch beam toward the big leather couch on the other side of the hall. There was a new shadow there, something more sculpted, shadow arms and shadow legs unfolding as it moved from where it had sat. The shadow walked toward them, slow, stumbling steps like a sleepy toddler. Baxter raised his gun and the torch, illuminating the shape and turning it from a shadow into a man.

The figure wore tattered sneakers and fingerless gloves and even before he reached up to draw back the hood of his jacket, Nikki heard McKenzie blow out a long, relieved breath.

"Jesus, Vince . . . " he said. "You almost got your face blown off."

Vince didn't answer him. He simply stood there for a moment, his arms hanging limply at his sides. Beneath the thin dusting of five o'clock shadow, his face was the colour of old plaster, his features . . . looser, somehow, as if there were stitches unravelling beneath his skin. His eyes were wide, unblinking, haloed with crimson, and something else about them struck Nikki as strange. In the glare of Baxter's torch beam, she would have expected his pupils to react, to shrink, but the black spots in Vince's eyes were huge, his irises a thin band of blue. His gaze touched each of them in turn, finally settling on—

"Baxter?" Vince said slowly. "Adam Baxter . . . "

"That's right, Vince," Baxter said carefully. He licked his lips. "It's me."

And suddenly Nikki realised something. Upon recognising Vince, McKenzie had lowered his gun. It offered her no opportunity to escape—McKenzie's long, powerful hand was still clamped firmly around her wrist—but even so the weapon was pointing now at the dusty floor tiles.

Baxter had also recognised Vince, but *his* handgun hadn't moved—it was still fixed squarely upon Vince's torso, Baxter's finger still resting on the trigger. Something was wrong, something in Vince's stance or maybe his voice was tripping all kinds of alarms in Baxter's head.

Nikki felt it too.

"Baxter . . . " McKenzie said. "What's wrong with him? He looks sick or something."

"Be quiet," Baxter told him, his voice soft but commanding. Then, a little louder, a little more relaxed, "What happened to you, Vince? I thought you were just going for a slash and coming back to the fun and games, and now here you are wandering around in the dark. What's going on, mate?"

"We've been waiting for you," Vince said slowly. "Waiting for such a long time."

It was Vince's voice, all right, but his speech was stilted, thick. It reminded Nikki of the final time she visited her father in hospital, the day after the massive, devastating stroke that would use up the last of him before morning. She remembered how the nurses had combed his hair into a side-parting, whereas Dad had always brushed it back, away from his forehead. Nikki had taken the comb and put it right, and she thought that he had tried to thank her, though his words were little more than a slurred jumble.

"Well, here I am, Vince," Baxter said calmly. He was stalling, Nikki realised, trying to give himself a few more moments to figure out what was happening here. "You look a bit green around the gills though." He nodded at the couch. "Maybe you should have a little lie down."

"A long time," Vince said again. "So many days. But . . . " He frowned, tilting his head slightly, as though listening to a voice only he could hear. "We remember it all. Every second."

"He's fucking lost it," McKenzie whispered to Baxter. "Gone loco on us."

"March fifteenth." Vince's red-rimmed gaze fixed on Baxter. "You told me I'd seen too much, so you cut out my eyes." He pointed at the grimy floor tiles. "I bled to death, just there."

Nikki couldn't see Baxter's face, he stood with his back to her, but she saw how his spine stiffened at Vince's words, heard a sudden, surprised thickness in his voice. "What?"

"June the sixth," Vince went on. "I died on the way here, in the back of the van. Heart attack, remember? Thirteenth of April, a Friday. Unlucky. I was still alive when you put me in the ground. It felt like drowning."

"Fucking hell . . . " began McKenzie. "Baxter, he wasn't even there that night, he—"

"Shut up," Baxter snapped, though Nikki wasn't sure which of his associates he was talking to.

"August tenth." Suddenly, Vince looked to McKenzie with blood-ringed eyes. Nikki felt him recoil beside her, heard something click dryly in his throat. "My birthday. You stabbed me in the neck. First of October. Bullet in the head—*pow*." His fist moved to the back of his skull as he spoke, drawing away from his scalp and opening as he mimed the mushroom of matter from his cranium. He glanced down for a moment. "These are my shoes."

"Fuck this," Baxter said quietly, and opened fire.

Nikki didn't hear her own scream. She'd never been in the vicinity of a gunshot, never seen anyone taken down like that, except for movies and TV and the news, and the sudden sensory input struck her before the shock. The sound was deafening, the muzzle flashed in the dark dazzlingly bright. A trace of burnt gunpowder that felt like a stifled sneeze.

She didn't see the bullet's path, of course she didn't, but for a heartbeat it seemed that she did, a slow-motion trajectory. She felt like her eyes could follow its heat-shimmering contrail from the barrel of the automatic to Vince's torso, and when it hit, it was as if some great vacuum had blossomed inside him. His middle seemed to *implode*, somehow, the grey material of his hoodie and the flesh of his belly sucked inward while in the same instant the wound erupted in a spray of crimson mist and charred tissue.

He flew back, as if yanked away from them by some invisible elastic fixed to his belt, his arms and legs jerking forward. He hit the desk behind him, striking it hard with the base of his spine—Nikki heard the desk's feet yelp against the tiles as the impact shifted it an inch or so across the floor. Vince's little flight ceased there, his body sprawled, his sneakers dangling a few inches above the tiles, his torso flat upon the top of the desk.

Baxter smiled, and said something, but Nikki couldn't make it out through the high, steady whine in her head. He walked toward the desk.

"—the fuck did he know all that stuff?" McKenzie said. His voice was muffled, as if she were hearing it from the next room, but he was closer to her, still gripping her wrist, and so she could just about hear him.

Baxter didn't answer. He reached the desk and brought his torch up to shoulder height, illuminating Vince's corpse. After a moment or two, he frowned, said something indistinct, " . . . wrong . . . never seen," then he beckoned to McKenzie. "Take a look at this . . . "

McKenzie tugged at her wrist as he moved to join him. Nikki shook her head, that whine starting to fade a little. She even heard McKenzie's shocked little gasp when he saw what his boss was suddenly so curious about.

Vince was stretched across the desk, almost spread-eagled, bleeding out onto its wide, yellowing square of blotting paper, like Alderville's final Rorschach Test. His eyes were open, staring sightlessly into the darkness above him. Steam rose in thinning clouds from his ruptured stomach, and in the torchlight Nikki caught a terrible glimpse of the matter within, a tangle of pulpy, purple-black organs. She wanted to look away, but the activity around the frayed, scorched edges of the wound captured her eye and held it.

Strands of grey, gristly tissue were twitching at the periphery of the breach, uncoiling, reaching across the maw to entwine in the middle like thin, eyeless snakes. Something of the tissue's sinewy texture made Nikki think of cheap, processed meat, intestines and eyeballs and genitals compacted and shaped into new forms. Another smell rose with the last of the steam from Vince's belly, something coppery and sweet and corrupt. The strands slithered around each other, twisting, knitting themselves together over the cavity. They looped and bound and entangled, sealing the wound like some grisly organic field dressing.

Baxter moved his gun nearer to the wound, and the flesh seemed to react, the thicker strings of it arcing upward to intercept the weapon. Baxter ignored them, and poked at the entwined tissue with the barrel of the gun. The repair tore a little under the pressure, the barrel slipping an inch into Vince's gut, but straight away more filaments slithered across to patch up the damage.

"Adam," McKenzie said beside her, and Nikki wondered dimly if he'd ever dared call his boss by his forename before. "I don't think that's a good idea."

Baxter didn't reply. He pushed the gun a little deeper, split a little more skin, and watched seemingly fascinated as the tendrils responded, caressing the barrel, tasting the metal like tongues.

Suddenly the tendrils tightened, coiled around the barrel, pulling the automatic through the tear and halfway into Vince's stomach. Nikki had no idea why Baxter let the gun go—perhaps it was shock, perhaps the strands were stronger than they looked, or maybe it was instinctive, a sudden fear that his hand would be pulled into the wound with the gun. Whichever it was, suddenly Baxter's hand was empty and he was lurching away from the body, some formless syllable of disgust escaping him.

And Vince sat up.

He swung himself gracelessly off the desk and stood. Baxter was backing away. He raised the torch like a club, its cone of light veering shakily toward the ceiling, then thought better of it, returning it to Vince as he walked toward them with stiff, stalking strides. Whatever monstrous horror show Vince had become, he seemed to decide, its approach was better seen than unseen.

McKenzie raised his pistol and fired. His hand shook and the shot went wide, sparking off the metal staircase behind Vince. McKenzie aimed again, using his other hand to steady his gun arm, and it was a few seconds before Nikki realised that he had released her wrist to do so. She was forgotten, at least momentarily. For McKenzie, there was only the thought of taking Vince—or whatever Vince was now—down. She glanced at her wrist, saw it encircled by a bracelet of bloodless white where his grip had been so unyielding.

Nikki turned to run, but before she could take a step Baxter was behind her, his big hand slamming down onto her shoulder. He jerked her back toward him, spinning them both around so that they faced the gunfight, his arm slipping around her waist to keep her in front of him.

"McKenzie!" He was keeping his skull low, tucked behind Nikki's head as much as possible, and his shout lanced painfully into her ear. "Don't just fucking stand there! Kill him!" Then, softer, almost as an afterthought, "*Again*."

But before McKenzie could shoot, the ground beneath them shifted somehow, rippling beneath her feet like a restless sea. Both she and Baxter stumbled, but he didn't let go. McKenzie took a surprised half-step to his left, and lost his aim again. There was a sound, too, a low, muffled rumbling, like some kind of explosion in the cellar. The quake only lasted a moment or two, but it was time enough for Vince to reach up to the stringy membrane that was keeping his guts in and pull out Baxter's gun.

It came free with a wet, tearing sound, thin ropes of grey mesh still sucking at the barrel—a trickle of dark blood and a watery, jelly-like fluid leaked from the wound before the strands entwined once more. Vince raised the weapon, and at once Nikki noted the difference between his stance and McKenzie's. Where McKenzie's hand quivered, Vince's was level and steady, his target acquired.

McKenzie saw that too and leaped to the side as Vince opened fire. He hit the ground and rolled, as the bullets meant for his heart instead blew fragments of stone from the wall behind him. Vince loosed another round at him, but McKenzie was fast, throwing himself into cover behind that big leather couch.

Vince swung his aim around to Nikki and Baxter. Baxter pulled her closer, angling his body behind her narrower frame as much as he could. She could hear his ragged breathing, was pressed so close to him that she could almost feel his heart hammering through his shirt, his jacket, his overcoat, and she knew that he didn't believe that a human shield would stop Vince firing any more than she did.

But Vince hesitated. He tilted his head again, listening to that internal voice. His lips moved, mouthed some silent response.

"That's right, Vince . . . " Baxter whispered. He backed away, pulling Nikki with him. "You don't want to shoot the nice lady, do you?"

They retreated another few steps. Behind Vince, Nikki

could see movement, a shadow rising from behind the couch. McKenzie. She wondered if Baxter had seen him too and was stalling again, until McKenzie could make the shot that might save both of them. She was disgusted to realise that she hoped his tactic would work.

"It's you we want, Adam," Vince said suddenly. There was a horrible, slippery quality to his voice, as if the workings of his throat and mouth were wet with something clotting and greasy. "But we will accept . . . casualties."

McKenzie was kneeling behind the couch now, his gun arm propped on the back of it, his free hand clamped around his wrist to brace it. The gun still shook.

Vince's neck tensed, snapping his head upright once more. Baxter kept guiding them backward. Vince's aim shifted, ready for a clean shot through the middle of both of them.

McKenzie fired first.

The bullet sheared off a slice of Vince's shoulder, a spray of blood and muscle. He flinched, and veered his aim away from Baxter to the new threat. The arm, barely attached to his pulverised shoulder, swung loosely as he turned, like meat on a hook, but he seemed unfazed. He started walking to where McKenzie crouched, firing as he went.

She saw McKenzie ducking as pieces of the couch and the wall behind him were blown apart, but then Baxter was spinning her around, seizing her wrist and dragging her across the hall, to a small office behind them.

As soon as they were inside Baxter shoved her away from him. He slammed the door shut, then quickly slid its bolts, one at the top and one at the bottom, into place.

"What are you doing?" Nikki asked. She was startled at how calm she sounded, and wondered horribly if she was going into clinical shock. "That's not gonna fucking stop him."

Baxter didn't answer. He hurried across to one of the office's two filing cabinets and dragged it away from the wall, pushing it over onto its side in front of the door. It landed with a hollow boom. Outside, Nikki heard another shot, as if in response.

He darted back to the other cabinet, and she expected him to drag that across to the door too—bizarrely she found herself almost moving to help him, an instinct to assist with the useless barricade—but instead he just pushed the cabinet a few feet along the wall. He swept the torch over where the cabinets had stood. The walls of the little office were tiled, she noticed, but there was an area here where the tiles stopped, forming a rectangle perhaps four foot tall and maybe a little less than the width of the two cabinets. She would have expected bare plaster, but the rectangle was filled with varnished wood, like a boarded-up window.

Baxter pressed his fingertips to the wood, gliding them along the uppermost edge, following their path with the torch. Beyond the door, two more shots rang out.

"The doctor who ran this place was a man after my own heart," Baxter was saying. "He understood that to climb the ladder, you have to stamp on the hands holding the rungs below you. You have to be ruthless to succeed. Fuck the weak, fuck mercy. And, whatever you do . . . " His fingers found a point perhaps halfway across the seam where the tiles ended and the wood began. He pushed. There was a soft click, and Nikki realised exactly what it was that she was looking at. "Always have a Plan B."

The door in the wall swung inward. Baxter crouched, pointing his torch into the shadows beyond it. Over his shoulder, Nikki could see some kind of narrow, brick-walled tunnel. Cobwebs quivered in a slight breeze.

"The clever old bastard had a few of these built into the walls over the years." Baxter stood. "Just in case the day came when the lunatics took over the asylum. It seems we've arrived at that point." He moved nearer to her. "Ladies first."

"What?" She shook her head. "Fuck off, I'm not going in there."

He grabbed a handful of her sweater. "You're coming with me if I have to drag you behind me by your fucking hair. As it is, I'd prefer to keep you where I can see you. Now move."

He shoved her toward the open panel, and she ducked inside. Baxter paused before following her though, looking at the bolted door behind him. She saw him lick his lips, watched his fingers twitch anxiously, itching for a gun, and realised with disquiet what he had already noticed.

The shooting had stopped.

CHAPTER SEVEN

THE SHOOTING HAD stopped a few minutes after Wren navigated his way out of the cellar.

He found himself in a windowless corridor and had followed the sound of the gunshots for as long as he could, but when the last echo died away he paused, unsure which way to go.

His hand hurt, but disquietingly less than he would have expected. It felt *cool*, almost, only vaguely connected to him, and he suspected that the nerves might be fried, dead to him now. Eventually, he dared to look at it.

In the torchlight, his skin looked like some blasted landscape, crimson and peeling. Pale, fluid-filled blisters were already rising. He could see strands of charred tissue never meant to touch the air.

Suddenly his knees unlocked, and he slumped against the wall. He felt a sob clawing its way up his throat and put his hand to his mouth to stifle it. His stomach rolled. His eyes were stinging, wet suddenly. They weren't tears for Markham, certainly, or himself, or even for Nikki. He thought they might be tears of shock, or horror, or of a final realisation that the thing in the cellar had been real, something alien and terrible in the real world of traffic jams and fish and chips and spiders in the bath, of hangovers and kisses and streetlights. The real world, the normal world, had been invaded. That thing in the cellar was a sight unseen, suddenly glimpsed.

After a moment or two he pushed himself away from the wall, forcing himself to take deep, calming breaths. He looked down at the gun in his hand, glad of its reality. Yes, he thought, the game had changed. But the most important rule had stayed the same. Kill or be killed. Survive.

Steadying himself, he wiped his eyes and moved on.

He took a wrong turn, finding himself in some kind of canteen, but he backtracked and after a few minutes he could feel gusts of chilly air streaming past his face. He headed down another corridor, remembering how cold it had been in the entrance hall when they arrived, recalling the shattered skylight. It did cross his mind that Alderville would claim a great many broken windows, and he feared that he might well be chasing his tail by pursuing the breeze, but in the dark there was nothing else for him to run with but instinct and the merest of clues. What else was he to do?

On the way, though, he passed a narrow window that looked out on to the front of the building and knew that he must be close. The cars were still there, meaning that the others, including Nikki, must still be in the building, somewhere. A short time later, he found himself in the wide, high room with its desk and forsaken IV stand, saw once more the place where he'd been betrayed.

Something cold touched his eyelid and he flinched, blinking it away. Another two chills brushed his face, one on his cheekbone, one on his lips.

He looked up. In the blackness above him he could just about make out the glow of five or six jagged wedge-shapes: the skylight. Bars of thin moonlight streamed down from the wedges, cloudy with swirling galaxies of snow. He wondered if it was past midnight yet, Christmas morning, and he remembered the gift he'd bought for Nikki, abandoned in a drawer at home, its shape unhidden by festive wrapping paper, still in the bag from the bookshop. It was a legal thriller, a genre he knew she favoured, but if he was honest he hadn't put much thought into it beyond that. He couldn't recall the title, or the author, or even if Nikki already owned a copy. The only thing he could remember about purchasing it was that he'd wanted something the girl he'd met on the train would like, the girl who had used a dog-eared ace to mark her page.

He looked up at the snow, the ivory signature of Christmas, and suddenly being apart from her felt like being a long way from home.

And when he looked down, he saw that he wasn't alone.

There were two figures a few feet in front of him. One of them was sitting cross-legged on the tiles, his back to Wren, his head bowed. The other was lying in front of this figure, face-down, legs splayed at an unnatural angle, the broken doll sprawl of the dead. Wren moved forward, some terrible dread encircling him—Nikki?—but as he approached he saw that the figure was male. Vince.

The other one was McKenzie. For a moment Wren thought he was dead too, but as he drew nearer, he could hear McKenzie's soft, even breathing. He guessed McKenzie could hear him too; he was edging forward as stealthily as he could, but to him his footfalls on the tiles sounded like they were echoing around the entire room.

McKenzie didn't turn, though. He seemed transfixed, totally focussed on the body in front of him. He didn't even twitch when Wren pressed the gun to the nape of his neck.

"Hello, Wren," he said.

Wren swallowed. He focussed on his hand, on the gun he held, trying to keep it from shaking, trying to keep himself from squeezing the trigger. He could feel the urge to kill McKenzie seeking to consume him, to eclipse his every thought. It would be easy to give in, deliciously so. Easy to fire, to end his life, to make him pay for what he'd done to him and to Nikki. But he needed him alive, for now.

"Where's Nikki?"

"I don't know," McKenzie told him. He made a small, dismissive gesture to an open door on the other side of the room. "The last time I saw her she was with Baxter, heading in there. But they've gone now. I checked."

Wren moved around in front of him to see what had happened to Vince, always keeping the barrel of his gun no more than an inch or two from McKenzie's skull, and as he did so he saw the weapon in McKenzie's hand.

"Drop the gun."

McKenzie didn't look at him. "It's empty."

"All the same," Wren said. "Drop it."

McKenzie opened his hand and let the weapon fall to the floor. Wren planted his foot on it and slid it back, a few feet behind him. There would be time to check McKenzie's claim that it was out of bullets later.

He glanced down at Vince and saw another gun clasped loosely in the corpse's hand. He knelt, reaching out to retrieve it.

"Don't," McKenzie told him. "Don't touch it."

Wren hesitated. "Why not?"

"Because . . . " McKenzie licked his lips. "Because there's something wrong with him. He's . . . infected."

Wren straightened. "Infected?" He'd counted two bullet holes in the middle of Vince's back, as well as the wide, ragged mouth further down, the one that looked more like an exit wound. He thought there were more, but the dark and the tattered, bloodied remains of Vince's jacket made it difficult to tell. If he'd had to guess at a cause of death he would have chosen lead poisoning rather than disease. "What do you mean? What happened to him?"

"Fucked if I know," McKenzie said sourly. His gaze never left the corpse. "We found him, down here, in the dark. He started saying things . . . weird stuff. Baxter shot him, point-blank, game over." He shook his head. "But the bastard got back up. He was gut shot, Wren, a dead man. But the wound, it just healed over, filled up with this . . . " He swallowed hard, pressing the heel of his hand to his brow for a moment. "This . . . rotten meat. It was like it was part of him."

I've seen it, Wren wanted to say, but he held that back. Admitting it to himself, allowing his mind to embrace that monsters were real, that was one thing, but saying it out loud . . . he couldn't, not yet.

"Baxter . . . he just took your girl and ran. Left me to it. I put every round I had into Vince before he stayed down." His brows drew together. "Where's Markham?"

"Dead." Wren told him. "What are you still doing here? The cars are still outside."

"Because . . . " McKenzie hesitated. "You didn't see him, Wren. I'm scared that—" He stared down at Vince. His bloodshot eyes glittered a little at the corners. "I'm scared that if I take my eyes off him, the fucker's gonna get back up and come after me."

Wren scowled. He wondered if McKenzie was having some sort of breakdown. Christ, he felt more than a little crazy himself. He thought of McKenzie sitting here for however long, watching a dead man cool, not even thinking to escape in one of the cars or even to check if Baxter—

Wren swallowed hard. A thought occurred to him.

"Have you got your phone?"

McKenzie frowned briefly, his eyes still fixed on Vince. "Yeah, why?"

"Because you're gonna call Baxter," Wren said. "You're going to tell him that I'm still breathing and Markham isn't." He considered for a moment, glancing down at Vince. "No . . . tell him you got Vince, but Markham is one of those things, too, now. Tell him he's on the loose, but I've found a safe way out and he can have it in exchange for Nikki."

McKenzie shook his head. "He'll never buy it."

Wren pushed the gun against McKenzie's temple. "Then you best work hard to convince him, hadn't you, Zachary?"

McKenzie nodded at Vince. "What about him? What if he—"

"He won't," Wren said. "And if he does, I'll make sure I kill you before he does. Now make the call."

His hand shaking, his eyes still set on the corpse, McKenzie reached for his phone.

***

They seemed to have been walking through the brick-walled passageway for hours, Nikki thought, though it couldn't have been more than ten, maybe fifteen minutes. She was leading the way, with Baxter whispering directions from behind her. He'd given her the torch, with a warning, "Try to use it against me and I'll break your fucking arm." Once again, she was struck by how he seemed to have an almost supernatural knowledge of Alderville's architecture, guiding them without hesitation, until they reached another panel like the one they'd entered through.

Baxter leaned forward over her shoulder, his fingers probing the top of the panel until he found the release catch, and was able to push the panel forward into another room. He ushered her forward, and as soon as the torchlight splashed into the space beyond, Nikki was startled by how colourful the room was compared to the endless grey she'd seen everywhere else in Alderville.

The light caught little diamonds of crimson and amber and violet, dazzling after the gloom of the tunnel. The torch was reflecting against two stained-glass windows on the far wall, and as her eyes adjusted she could make out a few more details . . . chairs, no, benches, one of them overturned, and something long and wooden and waist-high on the other side of the room. A table? No, as they emerged into the room, she recognised the object for what it was. An altar.

"The hospital chapel," Baxter said. "I've got some supplies here. Never knew when I might have to hide out."

He pushed past her, plucking the torch from her hand as he did so. He perched it atop the altar, angling its beam upward. Its thin glow cast coloured diamonds around the room. He moved around to the opposite side of the altar and brushed his hand across its edge, clicking another hidden catch. A panel sprung open, and Baxter leaned forward to retrieve something from within. When he straightened, he was holding a metal box, its surface black and polished beneath a thin coating of dust.

"Presenting Plan B," he said.

He placed the box on the altar and opened it, drawing out two automatic pistols. Nikki knew nothing about handguns, but something about the sculpted chunkiness of the weapons and the way Baxter was tilting them in his hands to let the coloured diamonds print themselves on the silver finish, told her that he was regarding this upgrade to his arsenal with a respect bordering on awe.

"The Eagles have landed," he said with a Christmas morning smile. "Let's see that fucker get back up after this," he said.

Nikki shook her head. "You're not going back out there?"

"Not by the same route, no," Baxter told her. "But yes, we're heading back. There's a couple of ways out of this place, but I want the one nearest the cars, so . . . " He lifted the pistols. "Round Two."

"What about Paul?" she asked. Her heart pounded high in her throat.

He paused. She saw something flicker across his eyes, the realisation that he'd almost forgotten about them, Paul and the other one, Markham. She had no doubt he'd leave them both here to die if he had to, Paul especially, but Markham was still one of his hired guns, like McKenzie, and could still be useful to him. And whether the weapons he held now would be effective against Vince or not, they both knew that Baxter was going to need all the guns he could get.

"I'm guessing he's dead," he answered after a moment, but she could see that he wasn't sure, was just trying to keep her scared, was thinking about Markham. Another gun.

He was reaching for his phone when it began to ring.

CHAPTER EIGHT

WREN HAD CHECKED McKenzie's claim that the gun he'd taken from him was empty and found that the bastard had been telling the truth. He thought about retrieving the pistol from Vince's cold, lifeless hand, but the word McKenzie had used—*infected*—made him hesitate. He didn't think whatever was happening here was some kind of disease—that thing in the cellar was no virus—but still, his instincts had insisted he disregard the weapon, and he listened to them.

He'd ordered McKenzie to move, to come with him to the hiding place he'd chosen, and when McKenzie had refused, terrified of turning his back on Vince, he'd calmly explained that if he didn't comply, Wren would be happy to club him unconscious and feed him a mouthful of Vince's infected guts, to see if maybe McKenzie might enjoy waking up as one of Alderville's dead things, a monster.

His eyes wet, McKenzie had nodded.

Now they waited in the little office adjoining the entrance hall. Baxter was coming. In the office, Wren had seen the open hatch that he must have used to escape with Nikki. It looked like it led to some sort of secret passageway. He didn't think Baxter would be coming back that way, it was too awkward, too confined, and he would be at a disadvantage trying to clamber through the hatch. When they met, Baxter would want his gun-hand free. Even so, Wren had half-closed the hatch and ordered McKenzie to drag one of the filing cabinets in front of it, not to block the opening, but so there was no clear line of sight between it and where they stood now, at the door to the office.

From here he could see both doors to the entrance hall. Whichever one Baxter chose, Wren would see him first. If there was a shot, he would take it. He had McKenzie stand in front of him, his gun jammed against the other man's head as an incentive against shouting a warning to Baxter.

Baxter was coming, and whether he believed Wren's lies about Markham and the escape route or not, this wasn't going to be any kind of civilised exchange. They planned to kill each other. That was the only certainty. Wren didn't have a plan, but his two objectives were clear. He had to save Nikki, even if he didn't make it out of here. And he had to kill Baxter, enough to know that the bastard couldn't come back. Nothing else mattered.

They waited.

Looking down on to entrance hall, Baxter immediately noted two facts. One: the centre of the room was dusted with snow, falling through the broken skylight. It lent the setting for this little showdown a strange, dreamlike quality. Two: Vince's corpse.

So, Vince was dead. Or as dead as he could be, anyway. That much at least was the truth, which made him wonder if Wren was being straight with him, about Markham, if nothing else? Something had obviously happened to facilitate Wren's escape from the cellar, and Markham becoming a zombie, or whatever they fuck these things were, maybe that had been the wild card that had allowed Wren to still be breathing and free and able to set this little trap for him.

It was a trap, obviously. You didn't torture a man and take his woman hostage, then expect him to hand over an escape route, no matter how much he wanted the bitch back.

He looked at the phone in his hand, recalling that alien unease he'd felt when it had rang back in the chapel. Yes, it had been McKenzie's name that had flashed up on the display, but he hadn't really expected to hear McKenzie's voice, had he? No. He'd expected to hear Vince, a dead man on the line, that thick, inhuman drawl. His unease had only deepened as McKenzie relayed Wren's instructions.

Wren would be down there now, waiting. Perhaps McKenzie was already dead, no longer in the game, no longer able to provide a distraction until Baxter got his chance to blow Wren's brains out. It didn't matter. He didn't need any of them, not now. He was Adam Baxter, and he was a survivor. He'd learned that truth from an early age, when his body had been skinny, and weak, and he had lain on his bedroom floor with the taste of blood in his mouth, the flavour of his father's wrath. He'd learned it when he realised he could endure pain, and the promise of pain, without fear, or tears. He had learned it when he was seventeen, bigger and stronger, the night he had finally slashed open the drunken old bastard's throat and watched him die. There had been no tears then, either.

He looked down into the hall and thought he saw Markham standing there, his abdomen unzipped, his death-slackened features staring up at him. He thought he'd seen Markham a few times on their journey from the chapel, sometimes reaching out from the dark, sometimes just watching them from the other end of a corridor. He hadn't told the girl.

He blinked, now, and Markham was gone.

He'd chosen his place well, an arched doorway on the gallery overlooking the entrance hall, away from the windows that would make his silhouette a target, close enough to the balcony to view the space below but distant enough to remain unseen by anyone down there. There was no sign of Wren, not yet, but it was only a matter of time. If he had to, he would go along with Wren's little game, at least up until the point he could take the fucker down. But not just yet. He wanted to try something first.

He glanced down at the phone and dialed.

***

Tucked away in his pocket, Wren felt McKenzie's phone start to vibrate.

He smiled.

"He's here," he said.

She's here, he thought.

Baxter glared at his phone's display for a full minute until the call switched to voicemail. He ended the call, cursing softly. It seemed that Wren was thinking ahead. He'd hoped that he'd hear McKenzie's ringtone, somewhere down there in the dark, giving him some idea where Wren was hiding. But it seemed he'd switched it to silent mode, and Baxter found the idea that Wren had even thought to do that very unsettling. He knew this was a trick, a trap, but even so he'd expected Wren to be at more of a disadvantage, stressed and injured, his mind in disarray. He would have to play this very carefully, he thought.

He dropped the phone back into his pocket and turned to Nikki. He still had her, the ace up his sleeve. Her eyes were huge in the dark, filled with fear and that hope he'd seen blossom in them back in the chapel, when she realised that Wren was still alive. One of the Desert Eagles was tucked into the pocket of his overcoat, but the barrel of the other sat comfortably in the hollow of her throat, ensuring that she wouldn't cry out some sort of warning. He had been very clear to her about that.

He pushed aside his concerns. Kill or be killed, that's all it was.

All he had to do was get Wren out in the open, and make his shot.

Wren's heart pounded. His arm, extended to push the gun against McKenzie's head, ached. But he could feel the adrenaline rushing through him too, turning his mouth to sand and his stomach to a hard knot, managing to feel horrible and exhilarating at the same time. He'd guessed that

Baxter would try his little trick with the phone, had *second-guessed* him, in fact. He felt some small sense of triumph, some hope that he might have a little control over all this.

Until he heard Baxter call out to him.

"Wren! You down there? C'mon, no need to be shy! I've got a lady here wants to see you!"

The shout had come from above them, from the windowed gallery bordering the hall. Wren peered up but there was nothing but shadows. *Shit.*

"Oh dear," McKenzie said. "Your plan gone a bit pear-shaped, has it?"

"Not yet," Wren lied. He licked his lips, his tongue like glass paper. Baxter's next move would be to draw him out into the open, demand that he show himself as a demonstration of trust. Give the bastard a clean shot.

"You're an idiot, Wren." He could hear the smirk in McKenzie's voice, the upturned lips of a smiling assassin. "He'll gun you down the moment he sees you."

"He will," Wren said. "That's why you're the one going out there into No-Man's Land to talk terms."

"Yeah?" McKenzie asked. "And what makes you think I won't run for cover as soon as I haven't got your gun stuck in the back of my fucking head?"

"Because." Wren pushed the barrel of the automatic a little harder into McKenzie's skull. "You know how good I am at hitting a moving target. You so much as fucking twitch out there and you're a dead man."

McKenzie laughed softly, and Wren half-thought he could feel him tilting his head back slightly, pressing his scalp more firmly against the gun, almost daring Wren to shoot.

"What?" Wren asked tightly. He wanted to pull the trigger then, to blow McKenzie's poisoned fucking brains out through his forehead, but he told himself, *Not yet . . . Not until you've got Nikki.* "You think that's fucking funny?"

"It *is* funny . . . " McKenzie replied. "It's funny because you think this is your trap for him, Wren, but it isn't. It's ours."

Wren opened his mouth to respond—*ours?*—but then he saw how there were shapes moving beneath McKenzie's clothes, shifting across his shoulder blades, uncoiling along the length of his spine, straining the seams of his overcoat, as if his torso was looped with snakes, roused now and stirring. There was something moving in his scalp, too—*beneath* his scalp. He felt it rippling past the barrel of the gun, jarring it slightly.

"It's funny because we could have killed you any time we cared to," McKenzie was saying. "But it's Baxter we want . . . for now, anyway."

A mesh of blackened, fibrous tissue was twitching from his cuffs, like the tendrils of that bad guy Wren recalled from the Spider-Man cartoons he'd seen as a kid, some sort of living costume, if he remembered correctly. The strands were entwining, quickly, wrapping themselves around McKenzie's raised hands like fleshy gauntlets.

The stench rolled into Wren, the wet, intimate stink of spoiled meat, of graveyards in the rain. It was as if every pore in McKenzie's body has been puckered shut but now they were opening, releasing the foulness of the thing inside him, and when he spoke again his voice was thick and silted, as though something was forcing its way up his throat.

"It's funny because you're too fucking late, Wren," he said quietly. "McKenzie's already a dead man."

He spun with an unexpected, inhuman speed, plucking the gun from Wren's grasp with one hand and striking a hard, slashing blow to Wren's cheekbone with the other. Wren staggered back, clawing uselessly for the weapon McKenzie held, but the other man was already turning away from him, spinning the automatic in his hand like a gunslinger, tucking it into his palm ready to fire.

He ran toward the stairs, firing up at the gallery as he went. Sparks flew from the metal balcony, and Wren heard Nikki scream. A window smashed. McKenzie was still firing as he reached the base of the stairs and bolted up them, two at a time, his overcoat billowing out behind him like some great black wing. There was movement on the balcony, two shapes. Baxter and Nikki.

Wren lunged for the doorway in time to see Baxter appear at the top of the stairs, his head thrust forward, a gun—no, two guns—in his hands.

McKenzie was five, maybe six steps away from Baxter when the blasts hit him. Wren saw the back of his overcoat shred as the shots tore through him, saw his shirt and the meat of his back erupt into crimson tatters. The impact plucked him from the staircase, sent him spiralling over the iron rail. He tumbled into the shadows, his unseen impact a thick, liquid thud.

"Baxter!" Wren shouted. "Wait! We can still—"

Baxter fired again, the shot tearing a chunk out of the doorframe. Wren threw himself backward and rolled, sliding his body into the cramped space beneath the desk. Baxter's next shot tore up the tiles where he had stood.

"The Eagles have landed!" he heard Baxter yelling hoarsely, his voice echoing around the hall. "Come out and say hello, Wren, you fucker!"

He'd shoved her aside as soon as McKenzie had made the stairs, tugging the other pistol from his pocket and swinging both of them up to blast him off his feet. The twin shots had boomed around the gallery, a nuke behind her eyes. Nikki staggered back, her senses reeling. At first she had thought that the figure firing at them, blowing pieces from the walls and shattering the windows, at first she thought that it had been Paul, until the saw the rotting, fleshy stuff lashing from his hands and pouring from his throat, and knew that it was another monster, not one like Baxter, but like Vince.

Empty shells sprang from Baxter's guns. They hit the floor and rolled toward her, smoking. Then she heard Paul's voice—"Baxter, wait"—and saw him emerging from that little office on the other side of the hall, and in the dark she heard Baxter whisper, "Gotcha . . . "

He loosed another shot, and she flinched, drawing back against the wall. Something crunched beneath her shoe. She lifted her foot and looked. Broken glass. A wedge shape, jagged and sharp, the size of her hand. The right size *for* her hand.

She knelt to pick it up. She could see her reflection in its tarnished plane—a grey, distorted stranger. Her hand wanted to clench around it, she found, wanted to hold on tight to the power it seemed to give her, but she didn't want it to shatter, didn't want the shards in her palm and fingertips. All the same, her grip was tight enough that little beads of crimson formed on its edge and ran across her reflection. She looked at the point, followed its lead like an arrow, and found herself looking at Adam Baxter's broad back.

He was shouting, cursing as he fired the guns again. He seemed almost to have forgotten her. She could do this, she thought, she could kill him. She could save Wren and herself.

She edged toward him, horribly conscious of the sound of her footsteps, but he was yelling and firing and she could do it, could plunge the glass into him. Not his back or shoulders, she considered. The wedge in her hand was perhaps a quarter of an inch thick, and she feared it would shatter before it could do much damage. No. She would thrust it into the smooth meat of his neck.

He fired again, still cursing. And as she raised the glass to strike, he started to turn.

She brought it down toward him, aiming for the surprise in his eyes, but he brought his arm down and batted her thrust aside. She swung the shard at him again, aiming lower this time, and the glass carved a deep, diagonal incision down his chest. She felt it scraping along his breastbone and bump over his ribcage, and when it reached the soft flesh of his stomach, it went deep. The glass exploded in her hands, a bright, shrieking pain. She screamed. Baxter grunted at her, his white shirt suddenly flooded with red.

"You bitch!" he spat. "I'll fucking kill you!"

He lurched toward her, raising one of his guns. He was

still between her and the stairs. She thought about charging him, trying to dart past, but she knew she wouldn't make it. She took a few stumbling steps back, into the corridor behind her.

Nikki realised she had nowhere else to go. She turned and ran, the gunshot hitting the wall where she had stood a moment before. Chips of stone flew like shrapnel, slashing at her face.

She kept running.

The shots from the gallery had torn through the thin walls of the office, exploding in a blitzkrieg of wood and plaster and stone. To Wren, it sounded as if a vast sack of bricks was being emptied on to the desk above him. Smoke and thick, choking dust filled the room. It burned in Wren's eyes, in his nose and mouth.

Then, somewhere within the explosions and the ringing in his head, he heard Nikki cry out. Not a scream, not really, more like a shriek of rage, some primal war-cry. A moment or two later there was another shot, but no more debris rained down upon the desk. Wren couldn't be sure, but he thought the quality of the sound was somehow different too, as if the shot was being fired *away* from him.

Another long minute passed, and Wren wondered if Baxter had run out of bullets, if he was reloading, or if he was just waiting for Wren to stick his head through the doorway so he could tear it to pieces. Either way, he had to take the chance. He scrambled to the door and looked out. He couldn't see any movement on the gallery, but that didn't mean that Baxter wasn't watching for him. There was only one way to know for sure.

Keeping low, he edged out of the office. He crept forward, certain that at any moment a bullet inscribed with his name would rip through the air and cut him down. He made it as far as the couch and ducked down behind it. His filthy shirt clung to him, drenched with sweat. His heart hammered. If

Baxter was still up there, he reasoned, then he would have found Wren an easy target at a dozen points between the office and the couch, but no shots had been fired.

He looked across at Vince's corpse, at the gun still clasped loosely in his dead hand. He could dive for it, but maybe Baxter was waiting for that, and Wren had no guarantee that the weapon was loaded. And behind that train of thought, he kept hearing the word McKenzie had used when he talked about Vince—*infected.*

Again, there was only one way to find out.

He moved quickly from behind the couch and toward the corpse. He kept glancing up at the gallery, but he knew Baxter wasn't up there, of course he wasn't. If he was, then Wren wouldn't have made it this far. If Baxter was still up there, then Wren would be—

He tried to stop himself thinking it, but he was too late. The words rose in his mind, sending a wave of almost tangible revulsion shivering through him.

If Baxter was still up there, then Wren would be dead meat.

He knelt beside Vince. He imagined himself taking the gun from his hand, imagined the pistol-shaped imprint it would leave in the snow. He reached out for it, and paused, his hand hovering.

Infected.

Wren shook his head. What the fuck did he have to lose? His fingers moved closer to the weapon.

"Stop," McKenzie said.

CHAPTER NINE

NIKKI RAN BLINDLY through Alderville's corridors. The place was like some hellish maze, nothing but doors that were locked or jammed, dead ends, passageways that took her back to where she started. No way out.

All the time, she felt like she could hear Baxter behind her, hear his laboured breathing, his lurching pursuit. Gaining on her.

He wasn't moving fast, his injuries wouldn't permit that, but she was beginning to realise that, as the prey in this chase, she was slowing down.

Her lungs felt sore and withered, too weak to make use of the air that she was trying to force into them. She was exhausted, aching all over. Her own injuries plagued her. Her hands were too hot, stinging, as though she was clutching a couple of naked razor blades in each fist.

She paused at a corner to catch her breath. She didn't want to, but her body insisted. She placed one hand against the wall and with the other she touched her face. Her hands were gloved in red anyway, so she had no way to tell if she was bleeding, but the skin of her cheek and brow felt rough and tender, peppered with chips of stone. When she drew her hand away from her face, it was shaking. When she drew her other hand away from the wall, it left a smeared, bloody print. She looked at it for a moment, remembering the brightly-coloured paintings she had created when she was a toddler, pushing her tiny hand into thick paint and pressing it to paper. Her mother had kept them, as she would have kept Melissa's.

Baxter's heavy footsteps, his strained, wheezing breaths. Not far now.

She ran again, and the next door she passed brought her to a room she recognised. The ward, or dormitory, or whatever it was. The place where she'd been held captive. Thin moonlight streamed through the room's lone window, through its rusting mesh. She ran for it.

She hooked her fingers through the mesh, not thinking about the metal cutting into her hands, not thinking about the fragments of broken glass sinking deeper into her palms, thinking only of the window, that if she could pull the mesh loose she could smash it, punch her way through it if she had to, smash the window and get away from him.

The frame around the mesh started to give, to pull away from the rotting plaster. Dust filled her eyes, making them burn. One screw popped loose, then another. She pulled. The mesh itself made a metallic creaking sound that she barely heard through her sobs. Blood ran down her arms, black in the moonlight.

Behind her, Baxter filled the doorway.

At the sound of McKenzie's voice, Wren froze. As he stood, slowly, he heard the voice again.

"You shouldn't have turned your back on us, Wren. That's the mistake that McKenzie made with Vince."

Of course. McKenzie had already been . . . what? Possessed? A zombie? Whatever the hell he was, he'd already been that way when Wren found him. It occurred to him that McKenzie must have been waiting for him. He'd known he'd escaped the cellar, known he was coming. Realisation struck him. All of them, the thing downstairs, Vince, McKenzie . . . they were linked somehow. Maybe . . . maybe Alderville wasn't besieged by monsters. Maybe, in some terrifyingly fucked-up way, it was besieged by just one.

He looked into the dark. McKenzie had landed under the gallery, behind the stairs. Wren couldn't see much, but he could see that McKenzie was still down, see that his arm was extended, see the blunt shape of the automatic pointing in his direction.

He glanced up the stairs. Nikki was up there, somewhere. He had to get to her, had to stop Baxter. But McKenzie could cut him down in a heartbeat. He had no choice but to go along with this, for now.

"Come here," McKenzie said.

Carefully, Wren advanced. Drawing nearer, his eyes adjusting to the gloom beneath the gallery, he saw that the angles of McKenzie's body where all wrong, his skeleton rearranged by the impact. Bloodied bone poked through his shins and one thigh. His arm, not the one holding the gun but the one he was propping himself up on, that arm looked like it was broken, too. But McKenzie was still leaning on it, seemingly unconcerned by the grinding purr of bone against bone when he shifted his weight slightly to track Wren's approach with the gun.

Baxter's bullets had hit him in the chest, face and neck, close range. When he swallowed, Wren saw something like frayed red string moving in his throat.

He should have been dead.

He is *dead*, Wren thought. *You know that.*

He had one eye left to him, a staring, blood-filled orb. The other eye was gone, along with most of his cheekbone and the top half of one ear. With no cheekbone to adhere to, the skin on that side of his face, probably shaved and scented this morning, had peeled away from his blasted skull like a slice of raw pork. It hung from his jaw, giving Wren a strange cutaway view of the workings of McKenzie's mouth. He could see the tongue squirming around McKenzie's remaining teeth. His tongue, and something else, a thick, grey shape like a tangle of worms. A tooth, not one of McKenzie's, forced its way up through his gums and jutted askew like a piece of bloodied popcorn. A second appeared. A third.

He was being repaired.

The grey tangle rippled in the cavity where his cheek had been and pushed a jagged fragment of bone into the space below his missing eye. The bone was jaundiced and cracked, far from a good fit, but when the tendrils reached out from McKenzie's face to stretch the skin of his cheek back over it, Wren was at least relieved that the cutaway view was gone. The empty eye socket filled up with a cloudy grey jelly, the best patch-up the thing could manage, it seemed. Wherever McKenzie was wounded, the grey matter mended and glued and stitched.

The gun never wavered.

"Jesus, McKenzie . . . what the fuck are you, now?"

"Not McKenzie, that's for sure." He chuckled bitterly. Blood and some thin, oily fluid bubbled on his lips. "Maybe Baxter's already guessed some of it, even if he won't admit it to himself."

He wondered if he could kick the gun from McKenzie's hand. He wasn't sure—every inch of his own body ached, slowing him, and before his injuries McKenzie had moved so fast, that weird, inhuman speed . . . Wren didn't know if he could do it, disarm the strange creature broken on the tiles in front of him, but he knew if he got close enough, he would have to try.

He took a step forward. "Admit what?"

McKenzie's lips twitched into a smirk. "That he knows what's coming for him."

"What do you mean?"

"We should be out there now, at peace." McKenzie gestured at the window. Wren licked his lips. There was nothing out there but the graveyard.

"You remember what Baxter said?" McKenzie asked him. "About Von Fleisher's experiments, about trying to make the patients see those . . . other places, the Twilight Zones?"

Wren nodded. He took another step, glancing at the window. *The graveyard.* His stomach felt like it was full of icy splinters.

"Whatever he did," McKenzie went on, "it messed with their brains. Sort of, switched them on, permanently. They never slept again, Wren. Even if they weren't mad at the start, they were fucking lunatics in the end."

Another careful step. "What's that got to do with all this?" McKenzie's good eye glared at him. "Didn't you hear what I said? He switched their brains on *permanently*. When he buried them, out there, their minds . . . their minds were *still* active, still feeling, still *aware*."

A drop of blood broke free from his eye and ran down his cheek, a crimson tear. "Their bodies rotted. The flesh peeled from their bones and they *felt* it, Wren . . . can you imagine what that's like? Even when their brains decayed, that wasn't the end. Everything of them, the agony and the madness and the terror, it bled into the soil, infected it. And when Baxter started throwing *our* bodies into *their* graves, it infected *us*, too. Our minds lived on."

Wren wanted to take another step toward the gun and found that he couldn't. He remembered the thing in the cellar, that mass of corrupted flesh, remembered how it had targeted Markham. Earlier, McKenzie had told him that this was *their* trap for Baxter, not his. It seemed impossible, all of it, but the pieces were slotting together now. Wren felt rather than thought the twisted logic of it dovetail in his numbed mind with an almost audible click.

"We grew, Wren," McKenzie told him. "We grew as if he were planting seeds out there instead of corpses. The broken hearts and the broken bodies. We planned. And tonight, with our murderers all under one roof, we saw our chance to get even."

"No," Wren heard himself say. "Not me. I didn't make this happen to you. And Nikki, she—"

"The woman was a surprise, yes," McKenzie admitted. "But you, Wren . . . " He raised the gun a little, levelling it as Wren's face. "Maybe you never killed us but you're guilty, all right. Guilty by association. Guilty as sin." He smiled, a patchwork collision of teeth. "And just so we have no misunderstanding here . . . *you* won't be coming back."

Wren looked at the gun. He wasn't close enough, McKenzie would shoot him down before he could reach it. More of that grey matter was twisting itself around McKenzie's hand, strands interweaving , covering it like a glove. Tendrils of it caressed the gun barrel, somehow tender and hesitant, threads coiling around the trigger guard.

And the gun began to shake.

McKenzie's whole arm was quivering. He looked at it, his single, blood-engorged eye widening. The grey tissue enveloping his hand rippled, like a flag in a gentle breeze.

McKenzie's head jerked left to right and back again, as though he was trying to focus on a dozen conversations at once. "No," he said, and although Wren heard *his* voice, there were other voices too, three or four of them unwinding from his throat, speaking in unison. "He's one of them."

The skin on his hand twitched and shifted, as if it were trying to unlock his grip around the gun, trying to draw his finger away from the trigger. Wren could see McKenzie fighting against the tremor. His brows had drawn together, his mismatched teeth clenched tight.

Wren thought about making a move, thought about going with his initial plan of kicking the gun from McKenzie's hand, but McKenzie's quaking arm was starting to fold, the barrel of the automatic veering away from Wren's face.

McKenzie's expression changed, edging from determination to something like surprise. He looked surprised right up the point when he jammed the gun beneath his own jaw and pulled the trigger.

For one terrible moment his head seemed alight like a Halloween pumpkin, the muzzle flare blazing from his eyes, mouth and nose. His skull expanded somehow, balloon-like, then deflated just as suddenly as its contents were vented. Wren threw his arm up in front of his face but still felt the hot droplets spatter his brow, his lips. One of McKenzie's stolen teeth clipped his hand. When he lowered his arm, the ragged, empty tatters of McKenzie's head had wilted to his shoulders, blackened and smoking.

Wren wiped at his mouth, his belly churning. The air stank of fried meat and gunpowder. As the smoke thinned, he could see ropes of the grey stuff writhing from the frayed stump of McKenzie's neck—they swayed blindly back and forth like sea fronds, looking confused, somehow, as if they had expected more to work with.

"Repair *that*, you fucker," Wren said as he reached for McKenzie's gun.

He recalled his hesitation to touch the gun that Vince had held, recalled that fear of contamination. He found no reluctance in himself now. He peeled McKenzie's cold, bloodied fingers from the gun and pulled it from his palm, hesitating only when he saw what the weapon had been concealing. No . . . this wasn't hesitation. He thought it was nearer to shock. For all his unexpected willingness to accept all this, the monsters and the dead men and the talk of Twilight Zones, he realised he had finally seen something that he might never believe.

The palm of McKenzie's hand was wrinkled and pale, soft to the touch when Wren pressed his fingertips against it. Gently, he ran his finger across the skin, smoothing out the folds and wrinkles. He traced the lines, as a fortune teller might, though he knew there was no future to be seen here.

The ink had faded with her skin, and one wing was torn at the tip, perhaps lost to the graveyard outside, but the butterfly was still as fine and delicate as when he had first seen it, four weeks ago. It had been nothing then, an incidental detail, but now it felt like a thing of great beauty in this desolate place, a thing for him and Nikki. It felt like hope.

"Thank you," he said softly. He remembered that Baxter had told him the girl's name. "Thank you, Caitlin."

He started up the stairs. As his foot touched the first step, he heard Nikki screaming. He ran, and as he reached the top, he heard the gunshot.

Baxter heard her footfalls echoing down the corridors ahead of him, fast at first, slowing as she grew weaker. He heard her sobs, her cries of frustration as she tried locked doors or ran down dead-end passageways. There were no such wrong turns for him though, he knew Alderville like he knew his own house, and he knew that for every second she wasted with a futile misstep, he would be advancing on her with certain, if lurching, strides.

He was catching up.

He wasn't in good shape though. He knew that. His stomach felt like it was flooded, full to bursting point, and that was strange, because when he dared to look down at himself he saw that he was losing blood at an alarming rate. His shirt, the front of his pants, even his shoes were soaked with red. The bitch had almost gutted him.

He knew he wouldn't see his daughters again. There was no love left in his marriage, but the thought of never seeing his girls again, their smiles . . . that hurt, cut him more than the glass in his belly. He would make the bitch pay for that, if nothing else.

He'd lost one of the guns, somewhere back in the corridors. He'd felt like something was sliding from the opening in his belly and instinctively let go of the weapon to place his hand over the wound, to keep whatever was slithering its way out in its proper place. He'd considered leaning forward to retrieve the pistol, but feared that if he did gravity would pull his guts out in loops, so he left it where it had fallen and moved on.

He found a bloody handprint on one of the walls. Somewhere close, he could hear some thin, metallic screech. The sound confused him. Below that sound though, he could hear her weeping.

He found her in the dormitory and understood the

screeching. She was trying to prise the mesh from the window. He smiled. That he was about to destroy her last hope of escape pleased him.

In the dark he thought he saw Markham again, and Vince, and McKenzie, all smiling at him with their death-slackened faces. There were other faces too, faces in the walls. The dead. The faces he remembered, the names he couldn't. He shook his head and the vision was gone. There was only the girl, turning to face him, her face twisted and bloody.

He brought the gun up to get her in his sights. His hand shook, but he wouldn't miss, couldn't miss, not at this range.

She shrank against the wall, weeping. It felt good to see her cower, to see the hope in her eyes replaced by terror and the absolute certainty that she was about to die. He might even have got hard, he thought, if his blood supply hadn't been such a rapidly dwindling resource. That made him chuckle, and the chuckle became a foul, coppery belch that felt like something inside him deflating. He coughed up crimson, spat it out, disgusted.

She was screaming now, screaming for Wren. He tried to speak, to tell her that no help was coming, but he couldn't seem to catch his breath. Silvery filaments twitched at the edge of his vision. He guessed that he didn't have long left, and his only wish was to ensure that she had less time to live than him.

His hand was still shaking, and he willed it to stop. Her screams felt like knives in his brain. At least if he shot her, he thought, it would shut the bitch up.

He squeezed the trigger.

CHAPTER TEN

THE CLOUDS SLIPPED apart like tired dancers, and wherever there was a window, or a skylight, the rooms and corridors of Alderville were filled with a cool, silver-blue glow. Wren hadn't even noticed, until he realised suddenly that he could see a trail of blood on the dusty floor, a trail that he could follow.

He tracked it, sickened, not knowing if the blood was Baxter's or Nikki's. When he found a sticky, crimson print of Nikki's hand on one wall, he felt sicker still.

He found Baxter first. He was sprawled awkwardly in a passageway, his back against the cracked plaster of the wall, his long, expensive overcoat pooling around him like oil. It was drenched in blood, frosted with dust and dirt. His shirt was soaked too, part-open, and Wren saw a wide, jagged wound in his belly, saw his pale organs twitching in the void. In the thin moonlight, his face was mushroom-pale, his lips a cracked, arid blue. His eyes were red-rimmed, unfocussed—Wren wasn't even sure if Baxter registered him as he drew nearer.

He had the barrel of his gun pressed hard against the side of his head, the skin of his temple wrinkling around it. He pulled the trigger.

An empty click. He let his hand fall into his lap. After a moment or two he looked up.

"Ah . . . Wren," he said thickly. "I don't suppose you have a spare gun, do you? Mine appears to have run out of bullets."

"Oh yeah." Wren raised his pistol. "I've got a gun for you."

Baxter didn't seem to hear him. He examined his empty right hand. "I'm pretty sure I had two before, but I must have lost one, somewhere in the corridors." He smiled, a shark's grin filled with blood. "Clumsy."

"Where's Nikki?"

His smile widened. "The lovely Nicola, of course. She tried to escape, you know. She might even have made it, too, if she'd had another few minutes. But she ran out of time. I saw to that."

Wren stepped forward. His brain felt like it might be boiling inside his skull. "Where?"

As he spoke, he noticed that the cracks in the plaster behind Baxter were lengthening, creeping out from behind Baxter's body like a spider's web. He thought he could hear something moving behind the wall, a low, slithering sound.

"I'll tell you where she is, Paul," Baxter was saying. Behind him, the slithering grew louder, like a rattlesnake hiss. "I'll tell you because all you'll find is another corpse, and I don't want you to miss a single fucking second of your miserable life after you see what I did to her. I want you to see her again and again."

The cracks in the wall were touching now, widening. Plaster dust drifted down on to the shoulders of Baxter's overcoat. Behind the cracks, Wren could see something grey and shifting.

"She's down there," Baxter gestured weakly along the corridor. "There's a dormitory." He chuckled. "You'll know it when you see it."

Wren looked along the corridor. He felt nauseous, too hot, like his heart was pumping lava into his veins. He saw that the trail of bloody footprints went on further along the corridor, beyond where Baxter lay now. His gaze followed them to the end of the corridor, where they turned sharply around the corner. But now he could see a *second* set of prints, moving in the opposite direction, and that track ceased at Baxter's feet. He'd killed Nikki . . . murdered her . . . then started back along the corridor, collapsing here. He turned back to Baxter, saw that he was still smiling. He didn't seem to have noticed the wiry grey tendrils uncoiling from the wall behind him.

"So," he said. "Are we fucking done here, Wren? Why don't you just kill me and get it over with? Send me to Hell." He laughed, flecks of blood spraying from his blue lips. "I'll be sure to say hello to that little bitch of yours and your dead kid."

Wren felt as if there were flames clawing their way up his throat. He lowered the gun. "No." To the thing behind the wall he said, "You take him."

The wall quaked, the cracks opening like a dozen mouths, rotted grey tongues unrolling into the corridor. One of them encircled Baxter's throat, squeezing. He opened his mouth to cry out and another plunged into it, a kiss from the dead. More of them thrust themselves into the wound in his belly, twisting around his bloodless innards and *pulling*, unhooking his organs from their moorings. He screamed around the dead meat in his mouth, a frail, choking croak. He stared at Wren, his eyes huge and imploring, and Wren thought perhaps he wanted him to shoot, to end his torture. Wren smiled and kept his gun down.

The flesh poured into him. The tear in his abdomen widened, unzipping him from genitals to throat, and still it filled him, the flesh and the rot and the earth and the spiders. His bones cracked, squeezed to dust. His eyes, still imploring, were pushed out from within.

Wren stayed until there was nothing left of him.

She wasn't in the dormitory.

He saw where she *had* been. On the wall, next to the window, he found a great spray of blood, smeared and streaked where she—where her body—had slid down the plaster. The plaster itself was shattered. The bullet had gone straight through her. Wren touched the bullet hole, the blood sticky and still warm against his fingers.

He closed his eyes for a moment, then set off to find her. He couldn't seem to let go of the gun.

She hadn't gone far.

He found her by another window. She had her back to him, looking out at the cemetery. The moon was high, painting the long grass with gravestone shadows that were lengthening, reaching out toward Alderville like black fingers. Baxter had been right about one thing, Wren thought. The cemetery did have a beauty all of its own, something raw and untamed. A dead place full of life.

"Nikki?" he said quietly.

"Stop," she said, without turning. "Don't come any closer."

Wren hesitated. Her voice . . . something in it *sounded* like Nikki, but the accent was wrong, not her warm Northern tones but an accent from somewhere else . . . London, maybe? And it was huskier too, almost hoarse, as though its previous owner had smoked to excess, or screamed too much. It was the sound of it, rather than the command, that made Wren stop. It turned his feet to stone, made them too heavy to lift.

"Nikki?" he whispered again, though he knew it wasn't her.

She turned, bringing the gun in her hand upward with a stiff, puppet-like motion. Baxter's gun, he thought, the one he'd lost in the corridors. He saw her injuries then, a terrible, frayed mouth in her middle, a gunshot wound that would have torn her guts to pieces, disintegrated one of her kidneys. Such damage aside, he thought perhaps the shock or blood loss alone would have killed her. No-one could survive that, not even his Nikki, and his heart broke there and then.

She had been repaired.

The hole in her middle was filled with a mesh of gristly tissue and tendon, woven through the edges of the wound. It didn't look like the forced violation that Baxter had endured, or even the improvised patch-up job he'd seen with

McKenzie. Somehow the injury looked like it had been mended with care, even tenderness. The mesh pulsed softly, he noted, like a heartbeat.

"No . . . " Wren said. "Why her? She didn't hurt you."

"Baxter killed her, not us," the London voice said. "We meant her no harm. But her body . . . her body is of use to us."

He felt his hand tightening around the gun. He wasn't afraid, but he registered how his index finger had made a slow, fractional slide from the trigger guard to rest on the trigger itself.

"Don't," the thing said. "We allowed you to live once tonight, Wren. That situation could change."

It looked briefly out at the moonlit graveyard, at its scattering of nameless tombstones.

"We want to make a deal," the thing said. "We're not giving her up, but maybe we can find a solution agreeable to everyone. It feels so good to talk. To walk, to blink, to taste the blood in her mouth. The flavours of living . . . so easy to forget. It's cold in the soil, Wren. Cold and so very dark. We want to feel the sun, smoke a cigarette, hold a hand. Looking through these eyes, within this exquisite frame . . . " It glanced down at its—at Nicki's body—but the gun never wavered. "All things seem possible."

The thing reached up to tuck a few strands of hair behind its ear, a gesture he'd seen Nikki do a thousand times. He felt the breath shuddering in and out of him.

"So, here's the deal," the thing said. "We take her now, and live whatever life we can, and you never try to find us. Accept, and you get to walk out of here. We think . . . " She hesitated. "We think perhaps Caitlin was right. We don't want to kill you, Wren. We have no quarrel with you, only with the ones responsible for our deaths."

"Fuck you," Wren said, and only when he heard the words catch in his throat did he realise he was crying. He raised his gun. "I'll be responsible for every last one of your fucking deaths right now."

The thing's lips drew back in a hard, terrible grin. "Okay . . ." it said. "It's your call. But you should know who else you're killing."

And the grin . . . changed, somehow, its edges softening. The moonlight touched her face, but the light in her eyes was something more, something human, and when she spoke again, it was Nikki. *His* Nikki.

"It's inside me, Paulie," she said softly. "All through me. Its thoughts and mine . . . it's getting harder for me to tell them apart. It's in my head, my mouth, my chest. It's holding my heart."

She placed one of her small, trembling hands on her abdomen, her fingers a gentle pressure. "It's in my belly," she told him. "I can feel it moving, it feels like . . . " Her eyes were wet. "Oh, Paul . . . it feels like kicking."

She smiled, Nicki's smile, and suddenly Wren felt like he was back in that void, the one he'd seen his body floating through on the television screen. Not a dream this time but a feeling, a sense that all the days ahead of them had slipped their moorings and were drifting away. It was like numbness and agony in one breath, in every breath, and it was more than his soul could bear.

His finger tightened on the trigger.

His hand was shaking but at this distance he couldn't miss, just one bullet, that was all he needed. The moonlight streamed through Alderville's broken windows, and all he could see was not what she was now, but who she had always been. The girl on the train who used a dog-eared ace to keep her page. The better half of Paul Wren, all that was good about him made flesh. He pushed, willed every last ounce of his strength into his trigger finger, but it wasn't enough.

Weeping, Wren lowered his gun and bowed his head. He could not look into her eyes, could not face the piercing coldness of her gaze. She would leave this place. He would die and she would live, but in the moments before she fired, he found an eternity to mourn them both.

ACKNOWLEDGMENTS

I'd like to gratefully acknowledge the care and support of the lovely people who, both personally and professionally, were an inestimable help in bringing this work kicking and screaming into the world. Thank you.

ABOUT THE AUTHOR

Roger Jackson lives in the United Kingdom, subsisting mainly on energy drinks and obscure horror and sci-fi movies. His work has appeared in several UK Small Press Magazines and radio programmes. *Cradle of the Dead* is his first novella.

Simon Kearns

DARK WAVES

Part One
Background Noise

1.

"I'LL BE HONEST with you, I don't actually believe in ghosts."

The speaker, Chris Henson, had stopped at the top of the stairs. His expression was guarded as he looked back for a reaction from his peculiar guest.

John Stedman said nothing and waited.

"Not since I was a child. I'm a rational man. My wife was a biologist." He turned to face the corridor and was quiet a few moments. He frowned at the far door.

"But there *is* something in that room." His lips wavered, an uneasy mix of defiance and distaste. "Something unpleasant. She felt it too. My wife. And I know there's a rational explanation, but that doesn't make it any easier to be in there."

"The room at the end?" asked John, stepping onto the landing. Eager now.

"Yes . . . It gets stronger the longer you stay in. I'll wait for you downstairs."

The older man descended and John checked the time on his phone. The ambient temperature was warm, average for a centrally-heated house. He walked slowly to the room.

"I hope it's a good one," he said quietly.

At the door, he took out a stopwatch, drew a deep breath, and entered.

The room was mid-sized, one of the smaller bedrooms of a typical 1960s semi-detached house. It had the look of having been a storage space for many years, a smell of dust and stale air. The air temperature was cooler, which was to be expected in a spare room where the radiator would remain turned off. Venetian blinds on the west-facing window tilted in a fair amount of late afternoon light. He shut the door and went to the centre of the room.

The far left corner was taken up by a chipboard wardrobe, white and slouching, on top of it a tartan suitcase, one clasp missing. Next to the wardrobe, attached to the wall, a mirror was half obscured by cardboard boxes. He began the stopwatch. A single bed lay below the window, neatly made up, but he doubted anyone had slept in it for years. On the south wall a ventilation shaft ran from ceiling to floor. Around head height was a small opening with a white plastic grill.

John slowed his breathing and closed his eyes.

From beyond the window came the faint yelps of kids playing football at the edge of the estate. Further off, a lawnmower, or power tool, rasping in long bursts. Eventually it stopped. He waited. Just as eyes adjust to the dark, his hearing settled into the relative silence. A low level hum became distinguishable and John tried to centre it in his attention, but it was elusive; indistinct and tremulous, it slipped in and out of earshot. His first impression was distance, perhaps an aeroplane, yet the sound did not diminish over time.

He moved his thoughts away from auditory sensations, concentrated on measured breaths, and proceeded, as much as possible, to empty his mind.

In the stillness, his eyes closed, hands open in front of him as if in supplication, John Stedman waited for something to happen.

And something did happen. A number of things happened. His heart rate quickened, his breathing became shallow. The skin on the back of his neck tingled. Hairs moved.

John nodded his head in recognition. He had travelled across the country to this estate, to this room, in the hope of experiencing these reactions, and here they were. His hackles were up and the sensory cortex was wiring nervy signals to get ready to fight or run, and he was smiling.

"Oh yes," he whispered, and paused the timer. One minute forty-seven seconds. Not bad.

He began to unpack his equipment.

In the living room the television was on, sound muted, but Chris Henson was not watching. His eyes were on the stairs. He regretted having invited this man into his house. Half an hour had passed and Chris wondered if he should go up, make sure everything was all right. Some people reacted badly to the room, one could never tell how it would go.

He stood when he heard the door of the room open. John came down.

"Good news, Mr. Henson. I think I can help you."

"Really?"

"I think so. I've done preliminary tests. If you like, I'll come by tomorrow with the rest of my kit. Shouldn't take too long."

"Shouldn't it?" said Chris, struck by the nonchalance of a conversation more akin to one he would have with a plumber.

"If all goes well, yes. One thing, though, I need to ask a favour."

"Oh?"

The homeowner became suspicious. The ad he had seen in the paper specifically stated no fee. Now this: a favour. What could possibly be asked in return for ridding him of this unpleasant something? If indeed it could be done.

John put his hands together. "I have a book coming out. In a few months. There's a journalist I know, he writes for a men's magazine. He wants to do a piece on my work and I said I'd let him know the next time I found something."

"A men's magazine?"

"*Prime*. It's a reputable magazine."

"And you want him to come here?"

"We can keep it strictly anonymous, if that's what you'd prefer."

Chris shrugged. "Would he want to interview me?"

"If you don't mind? It won't be a sensationalist piece. That's the last thing we want. I'm a professional scientist, Mr. Henson. I have a career besides this."

He considered. "Okay then. Bring him along, we can have a chat."

They arranged a time for the following day and shook hands. At the door, Chris gestured to the houses stretching over the hill.

"All fields when I was a boy. We used to play soldiers here. You move out of the town, but the town catches up with you."

John respectfully imagined green fields, nodded, and said goodbye. Walking away, he already had his phone out, the number dialled.

"Hello?"

"Matt, it's John."

"All right, mate. What's up?"

He looked back at the house. "I've found a good one."

2.

THE MIDDAY TRAIN from London was delayed. It lingered for almost twenty minutes next to a dilapidated warehouse on the outskirts of Leamington Spa. It clicked and hissed and sounded unwell.

Matt Kempton, his laptop open on the fold-down table, was staring at a photo of the man he would be meeting when the train finally arrived. They had spoken by phone a number of times but never met. The photograph was on the website of a regional newspaper and showed a tall, thin man in black clothes standing in front of a table laid out with electronic equipment. He looked to be in his late thirties. Below, a caption explained the scene: *Self-styled ghost hunter, John Stedman, displays some tools of the trade.* He wore unfashionably thick-framed glasses that did not suit his pale complexion. His dark hair, short and thin, was unruly. His demeanour, tight-lipped, somewhat haughty, was that of someone trying hard to be taken seriously. After a quick read of the accompanying article, Matt could understand why. It was very much tongue-in-cheek.

Matt clicked back to John's homepage and followed the link to his CV. The degree in Acoustical Engineering from Southampton had convinced him to take the man seriously. He looked over the rest of his resume: work experience with an architectural firm in London; a masters in Applied Acoustics, again from Southampton; a year's teaching at the same university; two years work on wind farms for a governmental agency; test engineer at the Fellows Academy of Acoustics.

With a lurch, the train began to move again. The warehouse, its broken roof and walls blotched with half-hearted graffiti, slid out of sight. Matt watched the littered embankment scroll by and wondered if he needed to call ahead. As he took out his phone, the train entered the station. John was waiting on the platform.

"Matt?" he asked coming forward, hand tentatively reaching out.

"John. Hello. Good to meet you."

The handshake was firm from both sides. Matt felt confident in himself, as usual. He was a handsome man, tall, gym-fit, with dark hair and a tan that looked to be regularly topped up. His attire was smart casual: designer labels, well-polished shoes. He wore an air of confidence and refinement like an aftershave, presenting very much the image of the *Prime* magazine man. He could have been from any of the adverts in the glossy publication, and he knew it.

"I'm parked just outside," John said.

The car was a shabby Volvo estate, mustard colour with highlights of rust. The inside was even untidier.

John lifted some files from the passenger seat and tossed them in the back. "I've been pretty much living out of this car for the past few weekends."

It took three turns of the ignition to get the engine started. He swung the car out onto the main road.

"How'd you find this place?" asked Matt.

"I put an ad in a local paper about a month ago. That's how I get most of my sites. At the moment it's all for free, I'm hoping that after a while, maybe if things take off . . . " He ended with a vague shrug.

"You think you could make money from it?"

"Perhaps," he said. "Television's where the money is. Once the book comes out, I'm gonna call some production companies."

They took a ring road that led them to the other side of town. The shops gave way to shopping centres. John turned off the main road and into a maze of residential streets. The houses were uniformly buff brick with white woodwork around the windows; a labyrinth of duplications.

He pulled up, and nodded to their right. "There it is. Number thirty-four."

Matt took in the semi-detached house, a caricature of suburban normality. For the first time he admitted to himself he was probably wasting his time. Two weeks ago, when John first contacted him, he had envisioned a quirky, thousand word piece on the conflict between science and superstition. A filler, scattered with phrases such as *anomalistic psychology* and *quasi-perceptual experiences*. Now, however, his article was taking on the form of a study in gullibility. Is this how your career ends? He asked himself in his editor's voice. The improbability of finding anything of mystery in number thirty-four, Mundane Road, was coming home to him.

"It's a pretty good one," said John, intuiting the other's scepticism. "The haunting."

"Yeah?" said Matt.

They got out and John took a bag and a laptop case from the boot of the car. As they neared the house, the front door opened and Chris Henson watched them approach.

"Good afternoon," said John. They shook hands. He introduced Matt, who asked if he could take pictures. Chris nodded, positioned himself in the doorway and folded his arms. Photos taken, they moved inside where tea was made and biscuits arranged on a plate. They sat in the living room and listened to the homeowner talk nervously and without aim for some time before Matt intervened by taking out a notebook, the sight of which stopped him mid sentence.

"Oh, don't mind this," said Matt, smiling. "May I ask you a few questions?"

"Yes. Absolutely."

"Great." He then took out a small recording device and placed it on the coffee table next to the biscuits. "Mr. Henson. Is your house haunted?"

Chris gave a snort of derision. "If you mean, is there a ghost in this house, the answer is no. There's no such thing as ghosts. Now, if you were to say, 'Is there some kind of unexplained event in the house?' I would answer yes."

"An event?"

"Yes. Energetic. Atmospheric. I don't know what exactly. That's what Mr. Stedman is here to find out."

Matt nodded, lifted his tea, and took a sip. There was a note of hostility in the responses he was getting. He wondered if it was brought on by embarrassment. Clearly the man wished to distance himself from the traditional lexicon of the uncanny.

"So you would classify it as an event, something well within the laws of science but as yet unexplained?"

"Precisely."

"Is there a history of unexplained events in the house?"

Chris took his own cup and held it awkwardly in front of his chest. "I've heard there are stories. I know one of them." He glanced involuntarily at the recording device, then went on, grudgingly. "These houses went up in the late sixties. Mostly for workers at the car plant. There was a foreman, his daughter, she was about thirteen at the time. This was the mid seventies. The room was her bedroom. Apparently she had some kind of breakdown. The family moved."

"That's it?"

Chris was defensive. "It was in the local paper. Poltergeist, they said. You can look it up."

"Do you know what happened to the girl?"

"I believe she spent time in psychiatric care. I don't know what became of her."

They all drank their tea. John took a biscuit.

"I hope you don't mind my asking," said Matt, "but did these stories have any consequence on the value of the property?"

He nodded. "Yes. Yes they did. That's how my wife and I could afford to buy. We were living in a terraced house near the town centre. Terrible damp. My business was in trouble. We found the idea of a haunted house laughable. The reduction in price was considerable."

Matt made a note. John ate his biscuit. They all drank.

"Have you ever tried a medium, or spiritualist?"

"No." About this he was definite. "People always said—you know, people came to the house and they noticed—they always said we should get someone in. A medium. We never did."

"Why not?"

Chris waved away the question. "I don't take those people seriously. There's a rational explanation for what's in that room."

"Did you ever try to find a rational explanation before now?"

"No one ever offered. To do it properly. That's the only reason Mr. Stedman is here. Why you're here; this is a scientific investigation. Of a—a tangible thing. A physical thing. A force."

He looked to John for reassurance.

"Yes. That's why we're here," John said. "Shall we go up?"

3.

CLOUDS HAD MOVED in overnight. The sky was low and the room duller than the day before. Chris waited in the hallway as the other two entered. Matt could tell his dislike of the room was genuine. His voice was controlled, but his body betrayed him: the way he stood to the side, ready to run; the manner in which he avoided looking directly into the room. As for his own impression, Matt considered it a dreary little space, piled up with boxes containing the not quite jettisoned parts of a life. The musty odour was synonymous with forgetting, with unconscious accumulation, spare things for a spare room.

"Right," said John, "we're going to do a little experiment. Stand here please."

He directed Matt to a spot near the south wall.

"Okay. I'm gonna stand with Chris in the hall." He moved out of the room. "Now. Close your eyes."

Matt closed his eyes.

"Just breathe normally. And wait. You have to give it a little time."

"Right."

"Just keep your eyes closed. And wait."

He felt them watching him. Breathing.

"How long do I have to wait?" he asked casually.

"A bit more."

He resigned himself to the game. Sighed. His shoulders dropped. Matt did not do this kind of thing, stand perfectly still with his eyes closed as others watched. He fought down the sudden self-consciousness and went to work. He paid attention to his body and realised, for the first time in years, how tired he was. His shoulders dropped further. He felt his legs give a little and found himself momentarily unsure of his footing. He took a deep breath but kept his eyes closed.

John glanced from his stopwatch to Matt. There was so much riding on what the journalist experienced it made the seconds drag. He willed a reaction, he demanded it of the room. With the three of them waiting like that, the flow of time slowed down, it thickened. Chris was leaning away from the room, staring at the floor with sad, nervous eyes. John tried to read the tiny facial movements of Matt, to discern his mood. Was that a flinch?

Matt kept his eyes firmly shut. A crease appeared on his forehead. It deepened to a frown. John couldn't tell if it was a good or bad sign. He looked to the man's chest to see if his breathing was affected. It had definitely quickened.

They waited. One minute passed. One minute twenty.

Determined to keep an open mind, Matt couldn't help but feel he was being set up. He was expecting some cheap trick to make him jump. As he was forming a verbal response to whatever was going to happen, he noticed a change in the air, as if his ears had slowly popped. He experienced an odd synaesthesia: he sensed movement near to him and simultaneously noticed a bitter taste in the back of his mouth. Swallowing hard, he concentrated on listening, convinced he would hear the sound of steps as they prepared the prank. Then, sudden like, someone was standing behind him.

He opened his eyes.

They hadn't moved.

"Sorry," he said. "I thought you'd—" He looked over his shoulder. "That's really weird. I was sure you were . . . "

One minute forty-nine. John grinned with relief. He smiled at Chris and walked into the room.

"It's common in hauntings to find what's called a centre.

A place where discomfort is at a maximum. That's where you're standing."

"You've got the spot all right," said Chris from the hall.

"But what's causing it?"

Matt moved away from where he had been standing. He looked nauseous.

"Infrasound," said John, with a certain amount of pride.

"You think I'm hearing things?"

"No, Mr. Henson. In fact, it's the opposite. You're *not* hearing things. Infrasound is a frequency of sound waves below our range of hearing. Below about twenty hertz. Just because we can't hear it, doesn't mean it's not affecting us."

He fetched his bag and laptop from the hall. Matt could see that John was enjoying himself now. Things were going according to plan. He imagined the feeling to be akin to that which a stage magician experiences when an audience member does exactly what is required; the set up had been flawlessly realised, now for the pay-off. Except this was no illusion. This, according to John, was science.

"You were right when you called it a physical thing. These sound waves, they can cause specific symptoms in anyone subjected to them. Headaches. Dizziness. Chills. Lower blood pressure, but a quickened pulse, which can bring on neurally mediated hypotension. There's a chapter about it in my book."

Matt had him repeat this last condition and wrote it in his notes. John spelt out the words.

From the bag he lifted an object about the size of a television remote. It tapered at the top to a thin silver cylinder. He switched it on and a digital display lit up.

"Another consequence, very common, is to imagine you're not alone." He turned to Matt. "You thought someone was behind you. You felt it."

"I can still feel it," said Matt, closing his eyes. "Even over here."

"I sometimes get it out here," added Chris from the hall.

"It's got a decent spread," said John. "But right there, at the centre, the sound waves are creating what's called a standing wave. They're bouncing back on each other from the walls of the room, reinforcing the peak energy in the centre."

He adjusted the settings on the gadget he held.

"So what's the source?" asked Matt. His camera was out and he was taking photos.

John pointed to the ventilation shaft. "I saw it as soon as I came in. Knew it before I took any readings." He lifted the object in his hand. "This is a very sensitive meter. It measures sound and vibrations. As I said, normal hearing stops around twenty hertz. This goes down to point-zero-five hertz."

He held it up. Chris had come to stand with them. They all watched the digital display. It settled.

"There. See that peak, the highest? That's the infrasound. Seventeen point seven hertz. That's pretty standard."

"You say it's coming from the air vent?" asked Chris.

"Yes. It could be the wind or a noise source outside. Imagine a bottle, when you blow over the mouth of it you can make a sound. That's what's going on here. This vent is acting like the bottle, but the vibration it makes is below our range of hearing."

Matt photographed the meter. He photographed Chris looking at the meter over John's shoulder. He photographed the air vent.

"Well then," said Chris, moving back into the hallway. He stood at the edge of the doorway, arms folded. "If you've got what's causing it. What can you do about it?"

John had opened the laptop and was starting it up.

"What's the top of the vent look like?"

"It comes out of the roof as a pipe. Has a grey metal cone."

"I'll need to get up there. First, I'd like to take some measurements. For my own records."

"Of course. There's a ladder to the attic. You can get up from there." Chris went off, muttering about a chair and the trapdoor.

John took from his bag a silver travel case. It contained a long, thin microphone. He placed it on a tripod and pointed it straight up into the air. Next out of the bag came a small black box with various dials and buttons. He identified this as a pre-amp and connected it to the microphone. The pre-amp was plugged into the side of the laptop.

"How can you work in these conditions? Doesn't it get to you?" asked Matt. He was leaning against the wall.

"Pinch your upper lip." John demonstrated. "It helps against the nausea. Earplugs can be useful. Stops the inner ear from getting too affected. As for the other symptoms, fear, depression and the like, I have a secret weapon."

So saying, he pulled over his bag and dug around in one of the pockets. Out came a two hundred gram bar of Num Num milk chocolate. He opened it, broke off a few squares, and offered them to Matt.

"Yeah?"

"It helps. Chocolate releases endorphins, which reduce stress. It's the best thing I've found to counter the effects of infrasound. I eat a lot of chocolate." He snapped off two squares and put them in his mouth. "Besides," he added, his voice thick with the stuff, "I love eating chocolate."

Matt pinched his upper lip and ate what he had been given. Even so, he went out to the hall and watched from there.

John started up a program on the computer and waves of sound undulated across the screen in green and red graphics.

When he had what he wanted, he asked Matt to keep an eye on the readings, picked up his bag, and joined Chris in the hall. The ladder was down. He climbed into the attic. With careful steps he crossed the attic floor to the Velux window, and hauled himself up and out onto the roof. The breeze was damp, off toward the city he could make out hazy sheets of rain, seemingly frozen between sky and rooftops. The buzz he had noticed the previous day in the room, the low level tone, was much clearer now. It was composed of lots of sounds, rising and falling, but overlaying each other to produce a drone. He cast around for the source but could see nothing. He took out his phone and accessed Google Earth. From his current location he zoomed out and immediately found what he was looking for.

Chris was waiting for him at the foot of the ladder. "Well?" he asked, somewhat doubtful, when John reappeared.

"I think that's it." He came down the creaking steps and into the room. He looked at the computer and turned to Matt. "What happened?"

"The peak disappeared."

John crouched down and tapped a few keys. "Yup. I'm just going through—yeah. That's it. D'you wanna stand back in the centre?"

Matt obliged. He closed his eyes. "Feels different."

Chris came to join them. "Really? May I?"

They swapped places. John began to pack up his equipment. After a minute Chris started to nod. "It's gone. My God. It's really gone." He laughed incredulously.

John lay the microphone in its snug, foam bed and snapped the clasps shut on the silver travel case. "I noticed the A46 runs near here. Any idea when it was built?"

Chris went to the window and looked out in the direction of the motorway. "It was before I moved here. Must've been around seventy-five or -six."

John nodded. "About the time the young girl lived here. The motorway is the source. You don't get it at street level, due to the embankment I guess. Up on the roof it's quite noticeable. The sound waves from the motorway were funnelling down the air vent, making a subsonic buzz. It was being piped straight into this room."

He zipped up his bag and stood. "I stuck a strip of gaffer tape across the mouth of the pipe. It hasn't blocked it. The dynamics of the air in the tube have been altered. No more infrasound. But you may want to figure out a more permanent fix."

Matt photographed the smiling owner of the house. He photographed him shaking hands with the smiling sound engineer.

The rain arrived half an hour later, as they got back into town. It thrummed on the roof of the car. John shrugged off the urge to reach back for the sound meter to find out the exact resonance. His guess was somewhere around 30Hz, similar to the lowest C on a piano.

Matt was busy with his mobile phone, texting. John waited.

"Impressive demonstration," said Matt at last, putting away his phone. "Does it always go so well?"

John thought back to the previous weekend. He had visited a house in Surrey whose owner was convinced it was haunted by the ghost of an Elizabethan soldier. After five minutes in the homeowner's company, John was pretty sure the whole thing was imagined. He felt nothing. His equipment found no evidence of infrasound. As he was explaining this, the man became aggressive in his attempt to convince John he was not making up the story. He was a thin, manic person who chain-smoked and had hygiene issues. The house was a mess, piles of clothes and newspapers, all over the place. He began to show John marks on his arm he claimed were caused by the ghost. John just about managed to stop him from taking down his trousers to display the scratch marks on his inner thighs. He followed him to his car, berating him for his lack of faith, his inability to help. The hectoring continued as John drove away. When you placed ads in newspapers offering to investigate paranormal events, this kind of thing was to be expected.

He used his arm to wipe the condensation from the inside of the windscreen. "Not always. Course not. Sometimes it's nothing to do with infrasound."

"Go on."

"Some places just have a story attached to them. That's often enough to invoke all the psychological effects of a haunting. Or it may just be a case of an unstable mind. The brain can do a pretty good job on its own."

Matt, who was recording the conversation, asked after few moments, "And what do you say to those people?"

John smiled. "There's a chapter about it in my book."

"Okay. I got my copy, by the way. Thanks."

"I'm bringing out an e-book as well, so . . . "

The rain thickened and the windscreen wipers struggled. "And the day job?"

"The day job. During the week I'm an acoustic test engineer at the Fellows Academy of Acoustics. Basically means I check out new buildings for noise insulation. We do a lot of industrial stuff."

Matt flicked through his notebook, pages crowded with observations he had made whilst in the house. *Spare things—dust—neurally mediated hypotension—nausea—chocolate.* The last word was heavily underlined.

"It's funny, the fact you eat chocolate while you work. I've read it's good for the heart, it can ease migraines, and obviously has psychological benefits. I'd never have thought it a cure for hauntings."

John nodded, smiling. "It's wonderful stuff."

The journalist shrugged. "I worked on a piece recently about chocolate. Three point seven billion, that's how much it was worth in the UK last year. Most of the cocoa comes from West Africa. They reckon nearly two million children work in the industry; more than fifteen thousand kids are trafficked and sold into it. Slaves, essentially, harvesting cocoa for high street names. Kinda takes the sweetness out of it."

John was frowning. "Children?"

"Yeah, sometimes they're sold by their parents, sometimes they're kidnapped. They send them out with machetes to climb cocoa trees and hack down the beans. Or they're spraying pesticides with no protection. Really young kids, you know? It's fucked up."

They said nothing for a while. John pulled up at the station. "What time's your train?"

"Half an hour. Thanks for the lift."

"No worries."

John held out his hand and they shook. "So, you'll be in touch. About the article."

"Absolutely."

"And you'll mention the book?"

"Yes. I'll mail you in a few days, when I have a draft."

Matt got out of the car. Before he closed the door, he bent down and leaned in.

"I'm going to see if I can find the newspaper piece about the girl. What do you think happened to her?"

"Can you imagine living in that room?" asked John. "Sleeping there, with those sound waves in your brain. All the time?"

Matt's face dropped as if the nausea the room had evoked came back to him for a moment. He swallowed it down.

"Jesus. No wonder she lost it." He shook his head and closed the door. From the station entrance, he waved goodbye.

It continued to rain. Clouds piling on top of each other had smothered the daylight. Cars had their headlights on and the world in his windscreen was like a surreal, bright night.

Before he drove away, John took his bag off the back seat. From the side pocket he pulled out the chocolate bar. He stared at it, taking in the brightly coloured bubble lettering, the image of the jolly parrot that was the company's logo. Remembering what Matt had told him, he determined to make sure he bought only fair trade in future. He bit off a mouthful and tossed the bar onto the passenger seat.

It was time to go home.

4.

TRAFFIC INTO LONDON was heavier than usual. It was almost nine by the time John found a parking space near his home. The rain had followed him most of the way but was stopped now, and the night was mild. In the flat the heating was on.

"John?" said a voice from the bathroom.

He pushed open the door. Catherine was in the bath, only her head visible above a blanket of bubbles. The heat from the radiator, coupled with the moisture in the air, gave the small room a tropical climate.

"Hey," he said, bent and kissed her. She smelt of peaches.

"You just get back?"

"Mad traffic, all the way."

A knee emerged from the foam. "How'd it go?"

He smiled. "Great. Couldn't have asked for a better one. The journalist loved it. The guy who owned the house loved it. Really great."

"I can see you're pleased," said Catherine. "Wanna join me?"

"I will. How's Brandon been?"

"Fine. He's got a cold again."

John went to his son's bedroom. He opened the door a crack and peeped inside. The five-year-old was fast asleep, snoring in a cloud of eucalyptus oil. His covers had been pushed aside, John replaced them and watched for a while. A nightlight on the chest of drawers projected little blue stars and turned them about the room. He left the door ajar and went back to the bathroom.

"I'm just going to my room . . . "

Catherine smiled. "I know."

At the age of six, John suffered an ear infection that changed the way he heard the world. It left him acutely sensitive to sound, as if God had suddenly turned up the volume on everything. This gave him an obvious advantage in his chosen profession, and it was especially useful for the work he was doing debunking hauntings. But it came with a cost. City living ensures a continuous background sludge of commotion and, for the most part, John was able to exist within it. From time to time, though, after long periods subjected to a repetitive sound such as that produced by motorway driving, or in periods of stress, he needed to reconnect with the sound of nothing. To this end he had designed his office.

It was a small room adjacent to their bedroom. Within, there was a desk, computer screen, surround sound speaker system, a few books on a shelf, and a rack of specialised sound equipment. On the floor, a largish wooden box contained the tower of a computer. The box had been built to completely isolate the sound generated by the machine. In fact, the entire room had been kitted out in such a way as to ensure the absolute minimum of external noise was able to penetrate within: the walls were insulated by panels of acoustic plasterboard with an inner layer of mineral wool. Furthermore, walls and ceiling were covered in egg box foam and the carpet was thick pile. Another outcome of this insulation was to render the room almost anechoic—devoid of auditory reflections, or echoes. With eyes closed, this created the impression of a silent space of infinite dimension. When necessary, John was able to additionally dampen unwanted noise pollution by means of a technique known as sonic masking. It involved emitting a particular sound, pink noise, which overlay and blanketed the unwanted frequencies.

In this environment, which he considered his acoustic

womb, John was able to switch off from the constantly present clamour that surrounds the modern human. Too long away from his silent sanctuary and he became irritable. Continued separation would leave him prone to depression. It was Catherine's contention that her partner suffered from a condition related to those found at the lower end of the autism spectrum: a susceptibility to sensual overload, in his case, aural.

Having transferred the data of the job just completed from his laptop to the computer in the box, he spent several minutes simply luxuriating in the neutral atmosphere of the room.

Feeling normalised, he returned to the bathroom and undressed. The water was pleasantly warm. Their legs slid against each other. They kissed. He lay back and sighed.

"It's good to be home."

The following morning, Brandon was up at half six. He launched himself onto his sleeping father.

John had been dreaming about a series of rooms. He was progressing through them toward an important meeting. Yanked from his sleep, his dream retreated; it lay down and hid at the back of his mind.

Over breakfast, Catherine recounted their trip to Epping Forest. Brandon had a new pair of bright red Wellington boots, which he had tried out the day before. He was wearing them that morning, pyjama bottoms tucked in.

"So, that's it for a while?" asked Catherine, meaning time away from home.

"Should be," said John, buttering the last piece of toast. "I needed a good one for *Prime*. We got it. The article should be out in time for the book launch."

He watched her reaction. John often felt his wife entertained suspicions about his weekend trips. *As if*, he thought. The idea of sleeping with another woman simply did not occur to him as a possibility. She had never said anything on the subject, and he didn't dare broach it for fear she thought him guilty. All the same, he was aware of a tension that crept into her voice when she spoke about his time away. Her eyes became restless. She was happy when he came back, but the day after she would wear a coat of peevishness.

"All right then," she said, rising from the table. "Brandon, eat your porridge."

When it came time for him to leave for work, John moved to kiss her. She didn't meet his kiss; she simply paused and allowed him to kiss her.

"You okay?" he asked, the door already open.

"What? Yes. Busy," she gave him a weak smile and went back to wrestling Brandon into his coat.

When he arrived at Fellows Academy of Acoustics, John went to the kit room and signed in the equipment he had borrowed for the weekend. The day passed without incident. Tuesday and Wednesday came and went. Catherine's mood evaporated, as it always did, its cause unspoken. Thursday afternoon saw him working in a newly constructed office building in Southwark. The job involved testing sound insulation through walls and floors as required by building regulations. The office block had been finished, but the rooms were as yet unfurnished and without carpet. He was alone in the five-floored building and would be for the rest of the day. The initial evaluation, the airborne test, was a straightforward procedure in which a loudspeaker broadcast pink noise at a high volume. John took meter readings in the same room, from the room next door, and from the rooms above and below. Pink noise has roughly equal energy in all frequency bands, thus allowing a full spectrum, quick and easy. He slipped on the large cups of his ear protectors and started the noise. Having taken the readings in the room with the loudspeaker, the source, he moved to the next office, the receiving room, and made a sweep with the microphone. The insulation was good. For a proper assessment, the procedure would have to be repeated many times. He went through the motions.

In the middle of the afternoon, the phone in his pocket throbbed. It was Matt. The journalist cut right to the point.

"I did a draft of the article and showed it to my editor. He liked it. In fact, he liked it so much he wants to make it a feature."

John's eyes widened. He set down the sound meter and walked over to a window.

"Wow."

"Yeah. Thing is, though, my editor wants to choose the haunted house."

"Okay."

"Same as before, we go to the site, you do your thing. We're talking five-page feature here. Professional photographer, the works."

John swore silently. He considered the best way to give an answer.

"Right. Yes. That *could* work. I mean, there's no guarantee the site you choose will be suitable. For me. I did tell you not every site has infrasound."

Matt was disappointed. "My boss was really keen you visit this place he knows."

"What is it?"

"A fifteenth-century inn."

John bit his lip. "Maybe I could check it out. Where is it?"

"Devon."

"Right," he said, grimacing. He was on the final floor, the fifth. A corner of the Tate Modern was visible. The reddish brick of the former power station stood vivid against the blue sky.

"Are you free this weekend?"

"This weekend? Um. I—I think so. You need it so soon?"

Matt was talking to someone at his end of the line. John waited. Five floors down, a bus was idling at the lights and he imagined he could feel the vibrations of its motor, channelled by the narrow street, with his palm pressed against the glass. Six or seven hertz at the low end, he guessed.

"Sorry, had to deal with that. What did you say?"

"I said, do you need me to go so soon?"

"If we want to coincide with the book launch—"

"Yeah. Uh, you spoken to the owners of the inn?"

"The Dawlish Inn, yes, I have."

John considered the proposal. There was only one problem: Catherine. Another weekend on her own. He pressed his forehead against the glass of the window and looked down to the street below. She would understand. A full feature. He took a deep breath and turned from the window.

"Okay. Mail me the address."

"Great. I'm sending the details right now. Talk soon."

That evening John picked up some things from the supermarket on his way home.

"I'm cooking tonight," he said when Catherine came into the kitchen. He was opening a bottle of her favourite merlot.

"What you got in mind?" She sounded suspicious.

"Beef strips in a creamy sauce, with fresh linguine."

"Sounds good. Brandon's got some rice and peas leftover. Just fry it up."

They ate when the child had gone to sleep. John was tempted to light a candle but thought better of it. The dinner was a success. As he poured another glass of wine for each of them, he told her about the call from the journalist.

"Devon?"

"I know, it's a pain. But a full feature. In time for the book launch."

She took a drink. Nodded. "Yes. It's good news. If there's infrasound involved."

"If. Yes." He swirled his wine glass by the stem and watched her. She was staring at her plate, expression neutral. "I was thinking I'd drive down tomorrow at lunchtime. Check it out. If it's workable, I'll stay the night. Get Matt down and we can finish by Saturday night. I'll be back on Sunday."

He noticed her eyes flitting.

"Catherine."

"It's Maggie's party on Saturday. We said we'd go."

He got up, came around the table, and hunkered down next to her chair. He took her hand and held it. "Darling, I gotta do this. For the publicity. You know I do."

Something in her face changed. "Yes, John. I know." She put her other hand over his. He bowed his head and kissed it.

"I'll go on my own," she said.

The dream came again that night, the series of rooms, the impending meeting. This time he had some intimation of the cause for anxiety: he wasn't ready; he hadn't finished something indispensable for the meeting, a report or some similar bit of paperwork. The rooms darkened as he progressed, the doors closed behind him and he knew they would not open again for it was impossible to go back. He wasn't ready and he needed to stop, if only for a moment, but on he went, against his will, running toward the final room.

He never got there, simply found himself awake and staring at the dim ceiling. With a sigh he turned over and moved his hand toward Catherine, seeking out bodily contact and reassurance. She flinched and murmured. His mind sought its own comfort—the book release was worrying him. *It is to be expected*, he told himself.

He closed his eyes and tried to ignore the sense that something else was bothering him.

Friday morning he was in the office writing up the week's reports in Southwark. He had spoken to his boss and, after promising to make up the time later in the month, been given permission to take the afternoon off. With regards to the borrowing of equipment, there was a problem. A handheld sound meter was fine, provided they weren't all being used. An omnidirectional microphone was not. The company owned five. One was in Ireland on a job. Three were on hire to a laboratory in Hampshire. The fifth was scheduled to be back but wasn't.

Despite the setback, John decided he would go ahead with his plan. With a handheld meter he could at least determine if there was infrasound at the site. He put a note on the equipment room door asking to be called as soon as the multi-field mike was signed in. There was one handheld meter left. He snatched it up and put it in his bag. At midday he tidied his desk and left.

Before investigating a haunting, John made sure not to learn anything about the site he was to visit, reasoning that to do so would influence his experience of the environment. All he needed were directions.

According to Google maps the journey would take around four hours. His destination, a village by the name of Little Banting, was just north of Barnstaple. He had to cross London, pick up the M4 all the way to Bristol, then head south on the M5. From there it was easy enough. The printer chugged out a copy of the map, with detailed directions along the left hand side. He made a sandwich and ate as he packed.

At the bottom of a note to Catherine he added an x and instantly wished he had capitalised it. Another sandwich was made, then he lifted the bag and laptop, checked for keys and wallet, and left the flat.

He took a large bite of the sandwich, placed it on the dashboard and put the key in the ignition. The car spluttered. He turned the key again. The car whinnied. He pulled the key out, kissed it for luck, and tried again. This time there was a barely audible whine. He swore and struck the steering wheel.

Ten minutes later, after much more swearing and many more attempts, he accepted it was not going to happen. He sat there, taking angry bites from the sandwich, weighing up his options.

Back in the flat he had his laptop out and was doing a

search for trains to the nearest station to Little Banting. The next available train left Paddington at five past five, arriving in Barnstaple just before nine. Checking the time, he saw he had three hours to get to the station. He booked a seat. It was expensive. Next, he searched his email for the message from Matt, got the telephone number for the inn, and called to let them know he would be late.

The main shed of Paddington Station clanged and echoed like a metal barrel beaten with a stick. John cringed as he entered. The high, wrought iron arches created a cavern of discordant noise. He put on his Bose headphones, sheltering his ears with an acoustic environment of their own. Even though the headphones had in-built noise reduction, he knew he could not drown out the ambience of the station without raising the volume to a dangerous level, so he selected something dirty and bluesy. According to the information screens, his departure was on time. Still hungry, he spied a Cornish pasty shop and gobbled a hot beef and Stilton.

When it came time to board, he joined the crowd of people being funnelled by the ticket gates onto the platform and into the sleek train. On entering his carriage, he removed his headphones to fully appreciate the long tube of quiet. His seat was found, bag stored, and with a hiss, the doors closed, further sealing the atmosphere of the train.

They made their halting way out of London, then gathered speed. The city gave way to longer and longer stretches of hinterland. By the time they were in open countryside, the October light had failed and the windows were mirrors.

Next to John, on the inside seat, was an overweight man in a navy suit, whose bulging thigh spread under the armrest and pressed against him. The man's telephone conversation consisted of explaining to a technically incompetent relative the resetting of a home alarm system. No, he said for the third time, you have to *hold* the button down.

John put his headphones on again and selected a gentle repetitive beat, suitable to the rocking of his chair. The music enveloped him, removed him from the public aspect of the train. He unfolded his copy of the *Guardian* and looked it over. Another humanitarian intervention was underway in another unstable state. Models were still too thin. Bankers still got bonuses.

He put down the paper, wearied by the catalogue of bad news. His thoughts turned to his stomach and the bar of Num Num chocolate in his bag, bought before boarding the train. He meant to get himself a fair trade chocolate bar, but there was none to be found at the station. Abducted children had helped produce his treat. He imagined his son, stolen from the flat, taken to an unfamiliar place and forced to work. The tears, the terror, the wincing from casual blows.

He had the feeling someone was watching him and glanced to his right. The fat man in the navy suit was looking at him with a perturbed demeanour, as if readying an accusation. John slipped off his headphones.

"May I get past, please?"

They were in Bristol. John stood up and the man squeezed out. The window seat remained empty as the train left the station. John moved into it. After a panorama of orange streets, the window went black again.

He lifted his newspaper, turned to the crossword, and began reading clues.

5.

FOLLOWING THE CHANGE at Exeter, John arrived at Barnstaple ten minutes after nine. On the road outside the station he spotted a taxi. The driver saw him and lowered his window.

"Help you?" asked the man, throwing a cigarette butt onto the tarmac.

"The Dawlish Inn."

"Where's it to? Little Banting?"

"Yes. Near the village.

"I know it."

"How much?"

"Twenty'd do it."

John sat in the front seat. The driver turned down the radio and steered the car through a U-turn and onto the road.

They sped out of Barnstaple and were soon in Braunton. From there they went north. The road became reduced to one lane bordered on each side by high hedges. Twice they met oncoming traffic which involved reversing and the finding of gaps.

"Been before, 'ave you?"

"No. Never."

"Holiday, is it?"

"Work," answered John.

The driver was quiet for a while. He drummed his fingers on the wheel. John felt his phone signal a text. He checked. The omnidirectional mike was back in the stockroom.

"S'pose you heard about the Dawlish?"

"Heard what?" said John, putting away his phone.

"They say it's haunted."

"Really?"

The man smiled. "There's more than just the one. There's a whole crowd of 'em up there."

John smiled back. "Sounds like fun."

After a few minutes they entered Little Banting. Other than a line of quaint cottages, there was a grocery shop, a pub, and another retailer, but he missed what they sold. They nipped through the village and took a right. The road climbed for about a mile, then they were slowing. On the right was an open gate above which, in old English script, a signpost announced The Dawlish Inn.

The car crunched gravel and drew up by the front entrance.

"There you go," said the driver.

"Thanks," said John and handed over a twenty pound note. "Have you got a card?"

"Sure." He opened the glove compartment and took one out. "I usually knock off 'round twelve. But if you give me notice, I can do later."

John took the card and slotted it into his wallet.

"Have a nice stay. And remember what I said."

"About the crowd of ghosts?"

"That's it." The driver nodded. "Sleep well."

As soon as he had closed the door, the radio was turned up. The car reversed out of the drive and shot off.

John turned and took in the building before him.

Part Two

The Dawlish

6.

THERE WAS A scallop main for table three, two salmon for table four, and another Irish coffee for the Artist in the snug.

Chef flashed his pan, blue flame for a moment, orange and white shellfish dancing within. Susan watched. The garlic, in a double punch, hit her nose and stomach simultaneously.

She tilted her head back and looked through the small window in the door to the dining room. Quiet night. Another sip of chardonnay. She could see Chef's cigarettes by the back door. The ring of the phone made her jump.

It was Kelly, calling from the bar. A guest had arrived.

"He's 'ere then."

"Who's that?" said Chef.

"Another bleedin' ghost hunter." With a sigh she opened the door.

The dining room connected to the bar by a low doorway. Walking through, Susan found her husband on his stool. Kelly was busying herself in an exaggerated manner behind the bar. She looked nervous. As usual. And the Olivers were in, at the far table by the fire.

The guest stood at the bar doing something with his phone. Susan disliked mobile phones. She disliked the way people used them. Kelly was banned from having one whilst working. Her own she regarded as a small cross, borne for her sins.

"Good evening, Mr. Stedman?"

The man was in his thirties. Unshaven. Dressed in black.

Black-rimmed glasses. Black bag. She was reminded of her cousin's boy. He immediately put his phone away, which scored him some points.

"Yes. Mrs. Colson?"

"Please, call me Susan." She went behind the bar to a small office at the end and took out a laptop. "Down from London?"

"Yes."

He went on to recount the problem with his car as Susan took his credit card and registered him.

"What make?" This was her husband, from the end of the bar. It was almost half-nine and William was surprisingly sober.

"Volvo," said John.

"Ah," he replied, as if this explained it all.

"My husband, William. An expert on bad cars." Susan handed back the card.

"Good evening." John nodded.

"So, you're here about the ghost?"

"There'll be time enough for that," said Susan, coming out from behind the bar. "First your room. And have you eaten?"

"I was hoping to eat here. I read some impressive reviews online."

"The restaurant serves until ten at the weekends." She led him up the stairs, reciting the menu. He was in room number four.

On the first floor landing she pointed out the King's Room at the end of the hall. "Henry VII spent the night. Fifteen-hundred and ninety-one. Now, your room's got a nice view onto the garden . . . which you'll see in the morning."

John found his room to be disappointingly modern. Susan named various items. Telephone. Wardrobe. Bathroom. In answer to his question, there was no Wi-Fi, he would have to go to Braunton for that. If it was an emergency she would let him plug into the socket in the office. She told him to come down whenever he wanted. He placed his bag on the bed and saw she really didn't like this; her expression made it clear that bags were for the floor.

"Actually," he said as she was retreating. "If you don't mind, I'd like to visit the haunted room."

"Before you've eaten?"

"I'm sorry. This is a professional trip. I need to do an initial test. See if I can work here. It won't take long. If it's no bother."

"No. No bother," she said, unconvincingly.

As Susan entered the bar with John, she instructed Kelly to see if Chef needed help. She waited until she was gone then stood by her husband.

"He wants to go in straight away."

William had a new pint. He turned. "Of course he does. And if he's going down there, I have to say, and I'm not being dramatic, you go in there, we're not responsible for what happens to you."

"Will," said his wife, with a glance at the couple by the fire.

"No. That's important. We need to say that."

John waited, trying to remain unobtrusive and eager to hear what they would say next. He was enjoying himself. The way people lived with a haunting fascinated him. This inn was old. Older than King Henry's time. There would be so many stories. So many lives had concentrated in this compact, low-ceilinged building.

"Have you had problems with people going in before?" he asked quietly.

She pursed her lips before answering.

"A few years ago we had a medium come in. My sister found her. She got awfully upset, this woman, kept saying, 'Too strong, too strong!' She tried to leave in a hurry, tripped on the steps, cracked her head open."

"I'm not a medium. I'm a scientist."

Susan dismissed the story. "The woman was unhinged. She should never—Just don't stay in too long."

She opened a door next to the office and flicked on a light. The stairway led to a cellar. "This way."

Stone steps. Big blocks, bowed in the middle from centuries of feet.

In terms of floor space, the cellar was about half the size of the bar area above. The ceiling was lower. Immediately in front of him when he reached the bottom of the stairs were the pumps for the beers. On his left, against the far wall, a tall fridge and a long freezer. Next to those were two washing machines.

"This is one of the cellars," said Susan and pointed to a doorless entrance behind him. "That's the room in there. I'll have a table ready for when you're finished."

"Thank you. I won't be long."

She smiled, checked a pump, then went back upstairs.

I hope it's a good one, said John to himself, approaching the doorway. Oh, I hope it's a good one.

Whereas the floor of the first cellar was cemented, level, and painted grey, the second was made up of dun-coloured tiles, irregular, some smashed, some missing, revealing compacted dirt beneath. The room was smaller than the previous one, the ceiling even lower, beams exposed. Barrels were stored here. Opposite, in the northern wall, he saw a chute going up to a ground level trapdoor where they would be delivered. A big iron hook was set into the wall above the chute. To the left was a large red object he recognised as a central heating boiler, oil-fired. Shiny silver pipes rose from it and passed through the ceiling. If there was infrasound in the room, this was a possible cause. It looked fairly new and as such would not be responsible for any historical haunting, but he knew that superstitions about old buildings could be reinforced by a modern infrasonic emission. Beside him, to his right, the partition wall between cellars held coils of ropes and hoses. Set into the eastern wall was a high fireplace and next to it an old poker machine.

He walked to the centre of the floor, be
and waited.

There was undoubtedly something pec
had perceived it as soon as he entered. Th
the air humid, and the ambience of the ro   ...giuated.
There was a dynamic quality to the air, an obtrusive element
that kept the molecules and dust motes sussultatory. The
boiler hummed softly, a low, extended sigh. His mind,
excited by the potentiality of the room, raced with thoughts
of success: a brilliant write up in *Prime* magazine, his book
topping the bestseller list, himself interviewed and—

He shook his head and closed his eyes. He needed to
concentrate. With renewed effort, he focused on taking deep,
regular breaths. As he relaxed, random images came to his
mind: the interior of the train from London, the equipment
room shelves, Catherine's face as she turned away, the
sandwich on the dashboard of his car. He let these pictures
rise and fall, and soon enough they stopped coming and his
mind was still.

His breathing pattern deepened. Somewhere in his head a
part of his intellect noted that the frequency of his brain waves
felt as if it had decreased from around 20Hz, normal alertness,
to the 8-12Hz, alpha waves. He was relaxed and in a wakeful state.

He thought of his son, Brandon, but he did so with a
feeling of sadness, of regret. He sought the cause of this and
remembered what Matt had told him about the child slaves.
His chocolate. He put the thought from his mind and went
back to his breathing.

In and out. Slowly, deeply. In until the lungs were full,
out until all the breath was expelled. He carried on, seeking
to becalm his thoughts with the meditative exercise. Still he
felt sad. He felt gloomy. Recognising this, the analytical
component of his mind perked up. Feelings of depression.
Despair. These were symptoms of infrasound. Trying to keep
excitement from hindering his impressions, he took a long,
deep breath and held it.

It was no good, his mind was flighty. He opened his eyes. There was definitely something going on in the cellar. He could feel it though he wasn't sure which of the five senses was informing this unease. The strange thought struck him that whatever it was going on in the vibrancy of the room, he would never find the root of it. Discouraged, he turned on the sound meter. There was a reading immediately, he pivoted slowly, the reading did not change, it was constant in all directions. 16.9 Hertz. He smiled, the site had infrasound. All that remained now was to identify the source and determine a means to shut it off. He looked back to the heating unit; it had to be the boiler.

At that moment the boiler gave a loud click and cut out. After the steady resonance of the machine, the silence that followed was weighty and sudden, it felt pre-emptive of something. He looked at the meter. The reading was still there, 16.9Hz, undiminished. It wasn't the boiler.

Turning again, he moved in the direction of the fireplace. He stooped down, stepped into the hearth, and held the meter inside.

The onscreen spike wavered. Then the screen cut out. He shook the meter. No response. The battery. He hadn't checked the battery when he took it from work.

As he was about to swear, all the lights went out.

Utter darkness. He froze. The smell of soot from the chimney made the blackness thicker. He stepped back but misjudged the edge of the mantel and knocked his head against it.

"God damn it."

His voice in the dark felt out of place, unfamiliar. He closed his eyes and listened. The cooling device of the pumps in the outer cellar emitted a mid-range drone; his own breathing was the only other sound. Yet there was still that anticipatory mood; a sensory clamour, putting his nerves on edge with a vague warning. It pulsed in his head like an artery.

With his hands he felt along the dust-thick mantelpiece and turned to the assumed direction of the door. He took out his phone and checked the signal. Only one bar. He rang the number for upstairs. The phone crackled. There was no answer; he let it ring.

With the same loud click, the boiler started up again and he couldn't help but feel it was mocking him.

His eyes were useless in the blackness and he closed them again to better use his other perceptions. Despite the fact that his thoughts were now tumbling over themselves in an attempt to explain his predicament, one thought was gaining predominance through repetition and forcefulness. It was an unwelcome notion, but the more he tried to repress it, the stronger it grew. *There is something down here*, it said, *something more than infrasound.*

Whilst thinking this, he heard a new sound. Footsteps. There was someone in the room with him, someone much smaller than him. This was not the imagined presence common to subsonic influence, this was a certainty; he had heard it. In his blindness he felt vulnerable. He hadn't explored the cellar properly. Obviously someone had been hiding the whole time. He strained to hear.

"Who's there?"

The pulsing in his head was increasing. He shrank away from the chimney, expecting any moment that a hand would reach out of it, take hold of his leg, his arm, his hair. Cursing internally, he wished he'd brought his torch.

"Hello. I know you're there."

He felt stupid. He was talking to an empty room.

Phone pressed to his ear, left hand out before him, he started walking toward the doorway, baby steps. He tried to calculate the distance. There was that noise again, more footsteps. And that was when a new thought entered his mind, either entered it or became apparent, as if it had been in him all along and only now he was admitting it. The thought was this: *I have finally found it.* What this meant exactly he did not know, but the seemingly innate integrity the idea possessed was undiminished. *I have finally found it*, his mind echoed. Disconcerted by the strength of certitude that accompanied this sentence, his brain reached for an easy rationalisation, namely that he had found a powerful example of infrasound—the one that would make him famous. Even as this occurred to him, he was aware of the cold dismay inherent in the knowledge that this was not the explanation.

He stopped moving so as to listen for further steps. Nothing came, and he started forward again.

The fingers of his outstretched hand touched cold metal.

"Jesus!" John yelped, recoiling. His breathing came in rapid gasps, his heart was racing. He extended the phone to see by its light. It was a barrel. His bearings were wrong and he had ended up by the barrels.

Just then, faintly, as if from very far away, a woman's voice spoke.

"Hello, John," it said.

He held his breath.

"Hello," said the tiny voice again, this time with some insistence.

The phone. Someone upstairs had answered his call.

7.

BACK IN THE bar, Susan was terribly sorry. It so happened that Kelly, who had been in the kitchen when John went into the cellar, was unaware he was down there. On coming back to the bar, she saw the cellar door open and the lights on. William was at the bar, Susan was in the kitchen. She did as she was always told to do, turned off the lights and closed the door.

They offered him a free drink. He asked what William was drinking.

"Bishop's Beard."

He had that. It was a dark ale, nutty and strong.

"Very nice," said John. Looking down, he realised he was still gripping the stopwatch in his left hand. The count continued, the split seconds spinning in their cycle, seconds and minutes amassing, as if tallying an unknown quantity within him, something the cellar had tipped into momentum, steadily building to a perilous conclusion. He pressed the stop button, cleared the digits, and shoved it into his pocket.

Eager to dispel the sentiment, he looked around for a topic of conversation. The barroom of the inn was cosy, typical of an English country pub. The ceiling was lined with dark beams, the posts at the bar hung with harness decorations in well-polished brass. Large, uneven slabs of stone made up the floor, and the bare stone walls held photographs of rally cars taken over a number of decades. William's, he supposed. The prints of pre-Raphaelite paintings he attributed to Susan. Framed antique brewer's posters filled the rest of the wall space.

"It's a lovely building. How old is it?"

William, who was about to take a drink, set down his glass. He straightened his back. He was a tall man, and he sat on a tall stool. "Most of the building goes back to 1447. In here, the front door, the rooms above us. And the meeting room. But the cellar and foundations are a lot older. The kitchens are now where the stables were."

It was a well-practised speech. He took a drink and continued.

"The inn was built by a man called Stephen Avery, a brewer from Barnstaple, who they say was an alchemist. Others say he was a black magician. Henry VII spent a night here. The King's Room, upstairs in the south wing. The inn was also used as a public meetinghouse. They had courts sitting here, executions even, in the yard. They kept the bodies in the cellar. Think about that, next time you're down there . . . "

He finished with a chuckle.

Susan shook her head. "Let's get you some dinner."

The scallops were delicious. For dessert he had three-berry cobbler and custard, and another pint. When he had finished, Susan invited him to join her at the bar.

The couple by the fire had gone home. Kelly was embarrassingly apologetic. John assured her it was not a problem. He suspected she had been an unknowing party to a practical joke.

"No, but, down there. On your own. First time an' all." She was late teens but younger looking, with an anxious energy that kept her hands moving. Cleaning glasses. Arranging the sink. Blonde, pretty, unsure of herself.

"Really. It was nothing."

"Oh?" asked William.

John took a drink of his pint. He positioned the glass on a beer mat. "Okay. It was uncomfortable. I can tell there *is* something down there."

"You've come all this way to tell us that?" William was exchanging a look with his wife.

"We know there's something there, but what is it?" asked Susan.

"Infrasound."

"In for a sound?" said William. "What, you mean like, a sound in an inn?"

John stared at him.

"No, Mr. Colson. Infrasound. It's a sound lower than you can hear."

"My hearing's fine."

"No. Lower than anyone can hear."

William took this in. "But if I can't hear it, how can it make me think there's something down there?"

John began a brief summary of the effects of subsonic frequencies, but he could not be brief enough. He could see the other's interest waning.

Susan listened closely. She waited for him to finish. "And can you do anything about it?"

"I should be able to. I haven't got all my equipment, and my journalist friend is supposed to be here."

"The man from *Prime*," said William.

"Yes."

The two men drank. Kelly, who had been standing nearby, moved closer.

"You can do something about it? What, like Ghostbusters?"

"Kind of. Except that it's not a ghost. It's sound waves."

Kelly shook her head. "Sound waves? No way. I mean, sorry an' all, but you won't be saying that if you stay down there any length of time."

"If you think you can help, you're welcome to try," said Susan. She took the bar cloth from Kelly. "Go and take the bins round. See if Chef's staying for a drink."

John excused himself and went outside. The night was cold and wet. The courtyard lay before him, closed in on three sides by the inn. Opposite, a large hedge and row of trees hid the building from the road. The rain was coming down in a persistent drizzle. He ran to the nearest tree, under which sat a picnic bench, green and slimy. He stood next to it and looked back at the inn.

The walls were white, made slightly orange by the two lamps hanging from the eaves. The downstairs windows were of the muntin style, small diamond-shaped pieces of glass, held together by diagonal lead frames. They glowed warmly. Here and there, bullion panes added to the antiquated feel. The low front door, of darkly varnished oak, was set beneath a sagging wooden portico. The windows of the first floor were smaller still, unevenly situated and unlit. An undulating tiled roof drooped over these upper floor windows, giving the whole façade a drowsy appearance. The two wings, north and south, abutted the central structure perpendicularly. The former included the kitchen and, on the first floor, more rooms. This north wing was modern in aspect, walls straight, roof horizontal, windows large and single-paned. The south wing, comprised of the function room and, upstairs, the King's Room, was shorter and clearly as old as the main building. Ivy covered its gable wall, draping the windows, very much in need of a trim.

The ground nearer the building was made of flagstones. Sitting upon them, two on either side of the front door, were picnic benches for summer months and smokers. Gravel made up the rest of the courtyard, continuing around the northern wing to where he imagined there to be a garage.

Although John was sheltered from the rain by the tree, fat drops occasionally fell from the leaves, patting his shoulders. He took out his phone, leant over to cover it, got Matt's number and called.

Whilst waiting for him to answer, he stared up at the black sky.

"John, how you doing?"

"I'm fine. Listen, I'm in Devon. At The Dawlish Inn."

"Good stuff. What's the verdict?"

"It's perfect. You have to come down."

"Tomorrow?"

"Yes. But I need you to pick something up. In London. The omnidirectional microphone I had before. I need you to hire it for the weekend."

"Is it expensive?"

"No. Not at all. I tried to get it from work, but it wasn't back in time. You hire it, I'll pay for it."

John gave him a telephone number, address and the full name of the item he was to pick up. Matt said he would be arriving mid afternoon.

Next, John called home. It went to answer machine. One of the raindrops got him squarely on the back of the neck and trickled down his spine, causing him to shiver. He listened to Brandon's high-pitched, halting message, informing him that no one could come to the phone.

"Hi. It's me. Sorry I didn't call earlier. I'm here, at the inn. Nightmare getting here. Car wouldn't start, had to take the train. Anyway. There's no Internet here, but my phone works, so . . . all's well. I'll talk to you soon. Bye."

He hung up and stared at his phone for a few seconds, wondering if what he had said was enough. It was relatively early, Catherine would still be up, sat on the sofa watching Friday night television, feet curled under her. Was she ignoring him? The home phone sat on a low table next to her end of the sofa and he pictured her, scowling as she listened to his message, deleting his message, going back to the television, her arms resolutely crossed.

When he went back inside his glasses steamed up.

"Cold out," said William.

"Yes," he said. He lifted his pint and took a seat by the fire.

Susan came over, picked up the poker and raked the embers. "We've had this place for five years now. We used to be in Maidstone. We had a pub there. We sold it and bought this place." She tapped the poker on the grate and replaced it. As she spoke, she kept her eyes on the fire. "We were told

45

it was haunted. It's well known for it. We've had paranormal investigators before. Nothing's ever changed, you see. There was a TV crew a few years back. American. They got very . . . agitated, whole lot of 'em. You remember that Will?"

"Eh?"

"The TV people. From America."

"Ah," he answered and chuckled.

John asked if they had a copy of the programme. She shook her head and apologised. He watched her as she stared at the fire. Her mouth was firmly shut, accentuating the creases around her lips that signalled her as a smoker. The muscles in her jaw kept tensing, like she was chewing. He got the impression she wanted to say something, but was stopping herself. He waited.

Kelly came back into the bar, the chef with her. Susan turned and got up quickly.

"Excuse me a moment." She went back to the bar, pulled Chef a pint, and poured a glass of white wine for herself.

To John's right was the large hearth, a small pile of neat logs on one side, and beyond that, the bar. On the wall behind him was a dartboard. The details of a recent game still visible on the chalky scorecard. JB had beaten SK in a prolonged game of 501.

To his left stood the wall that sectioned off the south wing of the building and the function room. The double doors had a plaque stating, *The Courthouse*. Directly opposite where he sat was the front door, flanked by an umbrella stand and coat rack.

Laughter at the bar. The Chef had been joined by the tanned man in a black leather jacket John had seen in the dining room snug. He heard him asking for a whisky by name. William said something and the man turned and briefly looked at John. He spoke to William in a low voice and they laughed.

Susan came and sat with John again. Closer this time. When she spoke it was almost a whisper.

"That's the Artist. He lives down the road. Spends half the year in Morocco. Paints all day, drinks all night." She gave him a what-can-you-do expression and turned her gaze to the fire again. The embers were fading but still gave off a decent amount of heat.

"I never hang around down there," she said, suddenly. "In the cellar. It gets inside your head. William says it makes his teeth sing. And as for Kelly," a roll of the eyes, "we don't even ask her to go in there anymore."

Her hands went to her hair, a thick mass of tight auburn curls scattered with grey. She gathered it behind then let it fall free again. It was similar to some of the pre-Raphaelite women in the paintings. She wore a thick coating of foundation and bright red lipstick, and looked to be in her late-fifties; at least a decade younger than her husband. She wet her lips before taking another sip of chardonnay.

"People say we should make more of the ghosts. That it's an earner. But I don't like to."

"Why not?"

"Doesn't seem right. Fair enough for those that come looking. But I'm not going to advertise it."

They stared at the embers. John frowned. "I'm sorry, did you say ghosts?"

She smiled. "Yes. Plural. There's more than one."

"How many?"

Her shrug was slight, her face blank, eyes still on the dying fire. "No one can say for sure. I know of three. The White Lady, the Hanged Man, and the Burnt Monk. The hanged man was a criminal, hanged for murder. Story goes he was innocent and now he haunts the cellar, howling for the injustice of it. The Burnt Monk was a seventeenth-century clergyman who, apparently, went down there to exorcise the evil spirits and ended up burnt to death by a mysterious fire that came out of nowhere and then disappeared."

John waited. When it was clear she was not going to continue he prompted her. "And the Lady?"

She turned to face him. Despite the make-up, he could tell some of the colour had gone from her cheeks. She had brown eyes, warm and rich around the pupil, giving way to a bluish grey at the outer edge. It was a direct stare but it didn't last for long, she glanced at his collar, at his hands on the table, then back to the fire.

"That's the one that frightens me. Nobody knows who she was. She comes dressed in white, her mouth open as if she were singing, or crying, but she makes no sound, just stands there, looking at you."

"You've seen it?"

"Her. Yes. But I don't wish to talk about it." She lifted the poker and disturbed the ashes, collapsing them.

John suddenly felt very tired. The heat from the hearth, the late meal, the strong ale. He yawned uncontrollably.

"Long day?" said Susan, standing.

"Yes. It was."

"Sorry again, about before."

She went to the bar and took a stool next to the artist. John finished his drink and brought the glass to the bar.

"Goodnight."

"You need a wake up call?" asked Susan.

"No. Thank you. I intend to sleep late."

His room was warm, the small radiator quite effective. A shower and into bed. He lifted his bag from the floor and took out the novel. As he did, the bar of chocolate fell out. He regarded it, remembering his resolution. No point wasting it, he reasoned, now that it's already bought. He bit off some squares and started reading.

Before long, he had eaten half the bar. He could have continued. To avoid doing so, he wrapped up the rest and put it back in his bag.

He read some more and his eyes got heavy, so he switched off the lamp and lay on his back. Whilst waiting for sleep, he thought about the building he was in. He located himself in relation to the ground floor and realised he was somewhere over the back of the dining room. This meant his room was, more or less, directly over the second cellar.

It occurred to him that he hadn't brushed his teeth, but he was far too comfortable to move. He drifted off to sleep with images of the subterranean room turning in his mind.

"Who's there?" he said, sitting up.

Silence.

With a stab of panic, and blinking hard, he realised he did not know where he was. The smell of the duvet, the darkness, the position of his bed. All of it was unfamiliar.

Then he remembered.

The room was black but for a slice of silver moonlight from the edge of the curtained window.

Muddled by sleep, John slowly came to the conclusion he had been dreaming. It wasn't the recently recurring dream, which was a relief. All the same, it had been an anxious dream, one of those vivid, half-asleep dreams in which someone was leaning over his bed. Someone short, dwarf-like, face hidden by the dark. It had been whispering. He could not recall any words but, in his mind, he could still hear the hiss of its voice.

As he stared at the floor, the line of moonlight disappeared. Someone had stepped in front of the window. Someone outside. With a chill, he remembered he was one floor off the ground. The room was entirely dark. Whatever was out there was trying to see in. He didn't dare move. Awful seconds passed, his teeth on edge, eyes wide, expecting any moment to hear that hissing voice again. The thin line of moonshine slowly reappeared on the floor.

He was about to put on the bedside lamp but decided against it. A quick glance at his phone told him it was nearly three in the morning. Throwing back the covers, he got out of the bed and tiptoed to the window. He warily drew back the edge of the curtain and peeked out.

A half moon hung above the trees that lined the small garden below. He saw now that clouds were trailing across the moon, occluding it, and he understood why its light had momentarily disappeared. He chastised himself for his initial reaction.

Looking down to the garden, he saw a greenhouse and a patch of earth that had been turned over then abandoned to weeds. A table, topped by a mosaic of spirals, was attended by three chairs of similar design, all of them made argentate by the moonlight. There was a low wall running around the garden and, directly below his window, a heap of large mossy stones had been piled up a long time ago.

Beyond the trees surrounding the garden he could make out the edge of the limestone ridge that ran north-south, beneath which the inn had been built. He remembered from Google Maps that somewhere to the west, on the other side of the inn, was the sea. The brightness of the moon and fast-moving clouds hid most of the stars. High up to his left he could see a very bright star. It didn't flicker and he supposed it was a planet. Probably Jupiter, he thought, then it too vanished.

He was thirsty. There was a mouthful of water left in the bottle he had bought at Waterloo. He finished it and got back into bed. The room was still very warm. An ache was spreading across his left temple. His head was heavy on the pillow and he could not get comfortable.

He made a mental note not to drink any more Bishop's Beard.

8.

THE FOLLOWING MORNING he ate a large breakfast. Eggs, beans, sausage and toast, cooked by Susan. The coffee she made was good and he had three mugs of it. There was one other guest in the dining room, a middle-aged, bearded man in walking gear. He ate muesli and drank tea as he read the *Times*. After breakfast he left with a walking stick and small rucksack, not to be seen again until early evening.

When John had finished eating, he went down to the cellar. He made sure both Susan and William knew where he was. Kelly started her shift in the afternoon. He brought his torch.

Despite the fact no light entered the cellars, John felt more at ease being there during the day. Whereas the first cellar was permeated with the low tang of beer, especially invasive for him on this morning after, the second cellar smelt of damp earth, of old rotting wood. Looking at the once-upon-a-time whitewashed walls, he noticed possible evidence of moisture around the corner where the poker machine was stored.

A thorough investigation of the room turned up nothing more than he had noted the night before. The boiler, a stack of barrels, the firmly closed chute, coiled ropes and hoses on the partition wall, a poker machine sat on a wooden pallet, and the fireplace.

Now that the boiler had been discounted, the most likely source of the infrasound was the chimney. Stood by the hearth, he tried to pick up any sensations of the subsonic waves. He felt nothing, other than a queasiness he put down to the mild hangover. The mantelpiece had a thick layer of grey dust. On it were three objects, a tablespoon coated in white paint, an old key, and a picture frame, empty of glass and picture. The sill itself was a thick piece of oak. He blew the dust from it and discovered at one end a pair of letters carved into the wood: *W.F.* He wondered what they stood for.

Very carefully he lowered himself under the mantel and inside the hearth. Using the torch, he illuminated the blackened walls of the fireplace. The metal back plate had a design on it, but rubbing at it did not budge the coating of ages old soot. He became aware of a throbbing sensation. It thumped, faintly. He experienced the first tremors of dizziness, a tightness in his throat, and with a grubby finger and thumb pinched his upper lip. He regulated his breathing to a balanced in and out, as slowly he set down the torch and put his hands out in front of himself.

He felt it. The waves of sound, throbbing. The sensation seemed to be coming from under him, or maybe it was funnelling down from the chimney, it was impossible to be sure for at times it felt as though it was coming at him from all sides. Maybe it is the chimney, he said to himself, reaching up inside with his hands. As he did, there was a movement to his right. He jerked his head to look. Then smiled. The sound waves were affecting his eyeballs, causing peripheral hallucinations.

There was no light visible at the top of the chimney. He wondered if it was blocked, and if so, on which floor. It occurred to him that, if he was correct, his room was two floors directly above, but there was no chimney in his room.

Again, movement, a pale blur, the suggestion of something white. His mind, primed by the conversation with Susan of the previous evening, immediately conjured up the White Lady. He ducked back to look. The room was empty.

"Hello?"

He waited. No answer, no movement. Turning to get back into the hearth, he saw again a pallid flit at the corner of his eye. Despite his familiarity with the symptoms of infrasound, he was perturbed.

Ready now for a confrontation, he twisted himself quickly. A sharp pain in his back told him the manoeuvre was a bad one. There was no one in the room. He scrambled out of the fireplace and quickly went through the doorway, expecting to find Susan or William at the pumps, or busy with a fridge, but there was no one.

He went back to the hearth and recovered his torch. There was nothing else he could do until Matt turned up with the omnidirectional microphone.

About half a mile to the east of the inn, at the foot of the limestone ridge, John discovered the Devil's Table. It was marked on the OS map borrowed from the inn as a prehistoric site; the local name had been supplied by William.

A megalithic ruin of some kind, it consisted of six large stones standing in an uneven oval around a central stone laid flat across two smaller ones. He stood on top of the horizontal slab and looked out toward the sea. The landscape fell away before him in a collage of fields and occasional trees. The sea, metal-grey and ribbed, was visible between two small hills, with the southern edge of Lundy squatting the horizon. To his right, in the middle distance, the village of Little Banting huddled in a dip. Behind him, the limestone escarpment rose like a tidal wave of pale rock. The grass around him, green, beige, and burnt, was rain-flattened and matted like wool on the carcass of a sheep. On the rim of the hill he could see a horse in profile, head lowered, unmoving.

The expansive ambience of open countryside intimidated John at a very basic level. In the city, sound was continually bouncing from a multitude of surfaces; it was always immediate, right in his face. And there was never any shortage of din: car horns, sirens, pneumatic drills, the buzz of traffic, the drone of airplanes, the ever present hum of the city itself. Out here, with such wide horizons, resonance did odd things. The sea, some two miles distant, pounded the air with wave after wave of momentum. Fast-moving clouds tumbled over each other, bouncing back vibrations from the sea and the wind. Seagull shrieks darted over the landscape, disembodied. Noises hovered, impossible to situate, snatches of sonic events from far, far away. He thought of his home office with a twinge of longing. It would be some time before he was able to reconnect with the consoling sound of nothing.

To distract himself, he went back to work and considered the sea as origin of the infrasound in the cellar, perhaps the reverberation of the waves, funnelled by the chimney, was responsible. He studied the landscape, the way the terrain rose up from the coast, and the location of the Dawlish within it.

Turning back to the shore, he experienced a moment of vertigo. Like his ears, his eyes were unused to the immense scale of it all. He squinted at the line of the sea, trying to pull it into focus, but it refused to comply, it blurred, it played tricks. The island of Lundy was to some extent defined, it was a rock to which his eyesight attached itself. Beyond the land mass, the sea and clouds smudged each other.

It started to rain. A heavy downpour. His trainers were already soaked from the wet grass, now the rest of him would be drenched. He went back to the inn.

As he approached the building from the rear, he could see two diagonal extensions of wall. They were buttresses. Once he saw this, he imagined that the entire structure of the inn was in need of support, that it was leaning, unsteady on its foundations. Between the buttresses were four windows. He determined his own to be the second from the right.

He took the path down the incline which, by way of a gate, led to the garden of the inn. As he entered, he saw that the wall surrounding the garden was made of two different types of material. The upper part was brick. The lower was constructed of stone blocks, the same limestone as the older parts of the Dawlish. Studying this bit of the wall, John realised that the garden had, at one time, been another wing of the inn.

Looking up at the back wall of the inn, the buttresses, his window, he felt the absence of the structure that once stood where he did now. The idea that the remaining building was unstable occurred to him again. He left the garden.

Around eleven he accepted the offer of a lift into Barnstaple with William. Susan gave him the name of a good restaurant for lunch.

William drove slowly but erratically, and John wondered if he was already drunk.

"Never thought I'd be living in Devon," he announced, ending the silence that had reigned in the car since leaving the inn. "Funny, how life does that. I'd always imagined I'd be in Spain by now. Lying in a hammock."

His nose was long, his eyes small and dark, cheeks sagging and fleshy. Away from the bar, in daylight, he appeared older than first guessed. His sparse, combed back hair was grey and wispy.

"What brought you here?"

He mulled on this for a while. "Couldn't think of anywhere else to go . . . No, that's not true. It was Susan. We came down on holiday and she loved the place. We had a pub in Maidstone. It was all right, I guess, but there's only so long I can stand Kentish people. Fourteen years I stuck it out. Meeting Susan was the only bright spot of my time there . . . You're not from Kent, are you?"

John shook his head. "I'm from Hackney."

"Ah," came the familiar reply. "We had it in our heads we'd open a B and B. While we were looking for properties, the Dawlish came up and we fell in love with it."

"Did the sellers tell you it was haunted?"

"Everyone round here knows it's haunted."

"What exactly is it supposed to be haunted by?"

William did an odd thing with his mouth, pulled the lips tight. He then relaxed them. "There's no definite . . . what, character? Historical person? There's lots of stories, some say it's the White Lady, others a monk, or a boy. Nobody knows."

The car had to pull into a gateway to allow a tractor to pass in the other direction. The driver lifted a hand and William waved back.

"What do *you* think about the haunting?" asked John.

"Me? Far as I'm concerned, it's an inconvenience. Kelly often refuses to change the barrels coz of it. Some people say it could be a goldmine, that we should advertise it as a haunted inn. I can't be bothered with it, and Susan won't. Her religious beliefs."

"She's—"

"Catholic. Not particularly devout, but she has certain ideas about . . . the soul."

"And what if I can get rid of the haunting?"

William laughed. "Get rid of it? It's a spooky old cellar. What's there to get rid of?"

They entered Barnstaple and William parked near the centre. An arrangement was made to meet again at three, then they went separate ways.

It wasn't long before John found a chain coffee shop and settled at a window table with a latte and his laptop. Catherine was not online. He sent her a brief message of love and hoped that her day was going well. Having checked his other emails, he opened Google and looked over results for local ghosts. One site had groupings for specific areas. He clicked on the Barnstaple link. The page that came up gave about ten locations and descriptions for hauntings in and around the town. There was no entry for The Dawlish Inn. Back on Google he typed *Dawlish Inn ghost*. The majority of results concerned a town named Dawlish on the Dorset coast. On the fourth page he found a relevant entry. The link took him to some text on the site of an American cable channel.

There was a summary of a documentary about haunted houses in England. One of the places visited was The Dawlish Inn, Devon, but no details were given.

Further refining of his search turned up nothing. He went to a sports site and read the results for the early kick-offs, then packed up his laptop and left the coffee shop.

Lunch was good, a serving of lasagne so large he couldn't finish it. He asked the waitress where he could find some books on local history and she gave him directions to his "best bet." He left a decent tip.

Tarka Books specialised in second-hand and local interest books. The name, John gathered, came from the book *Tarka the Otter*, which was based in the area. The man within pointed out the local history section. John browsed, but all the historical maps and references were limited to Barnstaple and its immediate vicinity. One book, *A History Of Barnstaple and Surrounds, From the Neolithic to Modern Day*, had an entry for the Dawlish, mentioning only that it had been built by Stephen Avery in the fifteenth century, and that Henry VII was said to have spent a night there.

John asked if they stocked anything on ghosts in the area. The man came over to the local section and scanned the titles. He pulled out a book; it was a collection of ghost stories from Devon and Cornwall. A quick look at the index revealed nothing on the Dawlish or Little Banting.

"What is it you're looking for?" the shopkeeper asked. He took back the book and placed it on the shelf.

"Anything I can find about The Dawlish Inn."

"The Dawlish? Down by Little Banting . . . No, I don't think we have anything. Have you tried the library?"

Barnstaple Library was a square block of a building, red brick, with an arched arcade on the ground floor. The woman at the counter spent some time checking the computer system. The best she could come up with were a couple of nineteenth-century maps of the area and a copy of *A History Of Barnstaple and Surrounds*.

With about three quarters of an hour to kill, John made his way back to the coffee shop. He bought another latte and passed the time on social networking sites. Catherine hadn't answered his mail, and she still wasn't online.

9.

WHEN HE GOT back to the Dawlish he found Matt at the bar, pint in hand. With him was a heavily tanned woman he introduced as Lisbeth, the photographer. She wore a navy body warmer over a green fleece, black jeans, and had blonde bunches emerging from a black woolly hat. She looked to be in her late twenties. An attractive face, blue eyes bright against her tan. She smiled, shook his hand.

"I just *love* this place," she said and he noticed an accent he couldn't place. "It's *so* atmospheric."

Perky, thought John. She leaned back against the bar and unzipped her body warmer to reveal a slim torso and full bosom. He couldn't help but think of Catherine—pale-faced, tired Catherine. This woman seemed the opposite of Catherine.

William, back on his stool, watched and waited for the pint that Kelly was pouring.

John realised he was staring at the young woman and his face reddened. He turned to Matt. "You get the mike?"

"In the car."

"Great."

Susan came in and introductions were made again. Matt and Lisbeth finished their drinks and went out to the car to get the bags. They were staying the night and Lisbeth talked excitedly about how beautiful everything was. Matt was simply happy to be in the countryside. He beamed and repeatedly took deep breaths of air, relishing its freshness and littoral aromas, rubbing his hands as if he were about to commence manual labour.

John took the silver travel case and checked its contents. Everything was in order.

"Shall we get on with it?" he asked. The others agreed. He went to his room and got from his bag a power lead for the laptop, a torch, his earplugs, and the last of the chocolate.

Downstairs, he made sure all the staff knew he was going into the cellar. He asked Susan for an extension cable, which she promptly produced. Just before John took them behind the bar, William cleared his throat and gave the same warning and disclaimer he had given the previous night. The two journalists listened, nodding. Then John opened the door next to the office and led them down.

"This is the bit in the movie when you shout out, don't go down to the cellar!" quipped Lisbeth.

Matt laughed. "It's okay, there's three of us. Just don't go down alone."

They arrived in the first cellar where John stood aside, indicated the doorway to the inner room, and offered them the way.

"Oh, it's perfect," said Lisbeth, entering the second room, immediately setting her camera to bring out the best of the low lighting.

Matt inspected the poker machine. "Jeez, we used to have one like this in my local. In Reading."

John had taken the laptop out of its cover and set it in the centre of the floor. He started it up, took out the microphone and plugged it in via the pre-amp. Lisbeth photographed him.

The relevant programme was launched and sound waves rippled onscreen. Immediately noticeable was a stationary peak to the left of the screen. He moved the cursor over the tip of the pinnacle and got a reading of 16.9Hz. To the right of this spike, the more common frequencies were illustrated by an undulating wave of smaller peaks. These represented the hum of the fridges from the other room, the pumps for the bar, possibly the boiler as well.

Carefully, he lifted the mike and moved it across the room

to the boiler. The background murmur of the cellar wavered at the bottom of the screen, and the 16.9Hz peak dropped in decibels. He moved toward the fireplace and the peak rose again. His guess seemed correct, it wasn't the boiler. There appeared to be a wave of 16.9 Hz emanating from the direction of the fireplace.

"Do you feel that?" asked Matt.

"What?" said Lisbeth.

"John. Am I imagining it?" He was still next to the poker machine, bemusement on his face. "It's the same feeling I got in that other house."

John smiled. "You're being haunted."

Lisbeth, frowning, approached her colleague. "What're you talking about?"

"Is this the centre?" asked Matt.

John shrugged. "I reckon it's actually coming from the chimney there, but you're near enough to feel the effects." He moved the mike and the signal stayed constant.

"What's going on?" demanded Lisbeth.

Matt took it upon himself to explain. He did a fairly good job, and made her stand where he had been, telling her to close her eyes. She did as she was told, waiting, eyes shut.

"There's this thing called neurally mediated hypertension," said Matt. He had obviously read John's book. "It's a common enough condition. It's possible that infrasound can bring it on. The symptoms include increased heart rate, but a lower blood pressure. It makes you feel dizzy, uncomfortable. It can even give you a chill. I mean, all the things associated with a haunting, you know?"

While this was going on, John had crouched down and gotten into the chimney. With the torch he explored the inside. About half a metre up from the mantelpiece, he discovered a hook set into the back wall. The hook would have supported a fireplace hanger, used to suspend pots over the flames for cooking. It was perfect for his requirements. To change the dynamics of the flue he needed a piece of scrap wood, a tape measure and a saw. He came out from inside the chimney.

As he did, Lisbeth opened her eyes and moved away from where Matt had placed her. "I don't like that," she said.

Matt took her place. "Weird, innit? I think this one's stronger than the other."

John stepped out from the hearth and watched the reporter. Matt's face took on an odd look. He put a hand to his forehead.

"Oh," said Matt. He became unsteady. "It's *really* strong . . . Oh shit, I think . . . "

The other two realised what was about to happen. Matt, panic in his eyes, made to run from the cellar, but there was no stopping what was coming. He vomited against the wall, next to the doorway.

"Oh God," he managed to moan.

Lisbeth, looking sheepish, stood beside him, unsure whether to put a hand on his shoulder, or speak, or do nothing.

"I'll get something to clean it up," said John and went upstairs. When he returned, Susan was with him. Matt had moved to the first cellar and was leaning against a fridge. When he saw Susan he moved to take the bucket and mop.

"Let me. It's my mess."

"Not at all," said Susan, walking straight through to the inner room.

"Oh my God," said Matt in a low voice. "I'm so embarrassed. It was that sandwich. From the garage. I knew it was dodgy."

"It's not your fault," said John and proceeded to explicate the visceral consequences of infrasound. Despite her tan, Lisbeth had visibly paled. The two listened patiently, and when John had finished, Matt excused himself, saying he was going to his room for a few minutes to freshen up. He paused on the stairs and asked John that nothing more be done until he came back, as he didn't want to miss anything. Lisbeth said she had some calls to make. There was no reception in the cellar, so she too went up to ground level.

Susan put her head through the doorway. "John, throw me some of those dishcloths, from the rack."

When she had finished cleaning, John went back into the second cellar. The smell of vomit mingled with pine-scented cleaning fluid and lay atop the fusty odours of the room. Looking at the scene, he tried to locate the garden above, figuring where, in relation to this cellar, the disappeared wing of the building would have been. He remembered the buttressed wall in the garden overhead and experienced an odd sensation, a shift, as if the room had very subtly tilted toward the wall that held the chimney. He regarded the other walls of the cellar, the shape of the room. The ceiling was lower in here than any other of the inn's rooms, and he couldn't help but feel there was an incline, that the floor itself was sloping toward the fireplace.

He studied the uneven back wall. The chimney looked newer, made of neater bricks. One stone in particular, to the right of the fireplace, between it and the poker machine, looked shaped. It appeared to have been carved, rounded, as if part of an entrance. The age of the place settled on him. The beams above his head, sagging, worm-holed, cobweb-hung, were close, bending down into the room, compressing the air. And the inaudible drone was ever-present, a spike he could see onscreen and feel in his head, his spine, and gut, and now his teeth also, for a dull ache had begun to announce itself somewhere in the squat row of lower right molars. He ran his tongue across the area, then clacked his teeth together. Although he couldn't hear it, he knew the infrasound was buzzing, low, low down, invisibly, silently, weighing in on his skull and his mind. He felt a rare but familiar unease, a building presentiment.

A few years previous, during an acoustics experiment in a chambered tomb in Ireland, he became convinced that the frequency of the sound waves his colleague was generating was going to cause the whole structure to collapse upon him. Shouting manically, John had scrambled out of the cave-like passageway, knocking over equipment and his co-worker. Somehow, in his haste, he had skinned three knuckles on his left hand, sheared the skin clean off. He wasn't aware of this at the time, and later, when he had calmed down, the sight of the blood was a further shock. The incident had marked him deeply; he had never before been so plunged into blind panic and irrational fear. The colleague referred to it as a panic attack and laughed it off. John never forgot it. The cellar caused him to relive the experience. It was the cold stone walls, the tightness of the space, the throb of infrasound in his bones.

Shaking off the feeling, he returned the mike to the front of the fireplace, went to his laptop and set the programme to record a sample. He watched the oscilloscope dance. Looking up, he couldn't help but be drawn to the corner where Lisbeth had been standing, in front of the poker machine. Something moved at the edge of his vision, he ignored it. It hovered, just on the periphery of his sight. All his senses told him it was getting nearer. Despite himself, he turned to look and saw a figure at his side. He reflexively pulled away.

"Jeez, man. Sorry." It was Matt. "Didn't mean to give you a heart attack."

John sighed. "It's okay. I've been seeing things in the corner of my eye. It's an effect of the sound waves. How you feeling?"

"Better." He didn't look it. "The old guy must have heard. He made me drink some whisky."

The two men stood side by side, looking from the computer screen to the chimney.

"Strong, innit?" said Matt.

"It is, yes. How did you find this place?"

"My boss knows somebody who did a piece on haunted houses. He said they'd visited lots. This one stuck in his memory."

John nodded. "I'm not surprised." He looked at his watch. "Want some chocolate?"

"No, but I need a smoke."

10.

KELLY KEPT AN eye on the door to the cellar. The bar was getting busy, most of the tables in the restaurant had been reserved, and Chef had his assistant. Susan was upstairs preparing two new rooms. She'd told Kelly what had happened, the man from *Prime* vomiting against the wall. When the two men came up she went straight over to them.

"What d'you think, then?"

"Impressive," said Matt.

"But, how does it come to you?"

"What do you mean?" asked John.

"I mean, like, how does it come to you. Have you seen it yet?" As she spoke, she carefully stepped between them and closed the cellar door.

"I've had flashes at the corners of my eyes. It's a common thing."

"You haven't seen it then."

Her tone was curt and dismissive. The two men struggled to respond as an awkwardness crept into the situation, as if they felt themselves judged by the young woman, found wanting.

John was about to speak when Susan's voice cut through the murmur of the bar.

"Kelly, I think Mr. Oliver would like another pint."

The girl slipped away.

"Everything okay now?" said Susan. "Good," she continued before they could answer. "It's a Saturday; we're going to be busy. When do you think you'd like to eat?"

"Seven? Eight?" said John, looking to Matt.

"Half seven, then. Chef's found some wonderful guinea fowl."

She opened the door to her office.

"Actually, Susan," said John. "I'm going to need a few things, a saw, a piece of scrap wood."

She smiled. "That's my husband's department. Excuse me." She went inside.

William was at the bar, on his stool. When John explained what he needed, the older man slapped his thighs with his hands.

"That, I *can* do." He got down from his stool. "Come with me."

They passed through the kitchen to a small yard with a garage and a shed. William went over to the shed, pulled a sizeable bunch of keys from his pocket and began going through them. When he had the right one, he opened the door and went inside. John followed him.

One side the shed was piled high with tables and chairs, messily stacked, with rolls of carpet up against them. A couple of mattresses lay across the top of the heap. The other side was bare with a work bench running the length of the wall. William pointed to beneath the bench.

"There's off-cuts of wood down there. What size you after?"

John explained. They soon found a piece of chipboard that looked about right. John took out his tape measure and confirmed. It was just over his requirements. William handed him a saw from a hook on the wall.

"Do you ever light the fire in the cellar?"

William shook his head. "Never have."

"Okay. Good. I'm going to block up the chimney with this piece of wood. Best you know I've done that."

William regarded him with a quizzical look but said nothing.

Back in the cellar, he put the wood and saw next to the fireplace. The power of the infrasound seemed to be getting stronger, a phenomenon he put down to it having a cumulative effect. He took out the chocolate bar. There were only four squares left. He ate them greedily.

"I'm gonna need more of that," he said aloud. There was movement in the corner of his eye. Involuntarily, he glanced in that direction and something odd happened. As he turned his head, his vision picked up a fluttering at its edges, the usual repercussion of the subsonic waves on the eyeballs. But there was something else. Whilst in movement, his eyes had registered a figure in the centre of the room. When he looked directly at that part of the cellar, there was nothing to be seen. It was only when his sight was panning from one side to the other that the shape was visible. It appeared to be human, short in stature, like a dwarf or a child. He stepped away from the chimney, toward the poker machine, continually turning his head from side to side. The faster he shook his head, the clearer the outline became, and for a few moments he had the impression he was seeing it in detail. It was about three feet high, very dark, as if hidden in shadow, and although no features were perceptible, he could tell it was facing him. It was looking at him. John became woozy with the effort of shaking his head and had to stop. His vision swam and he feared he was about to pass out. He blinked hard and the body of the nanus was briefly vivid, a visual echo, before it dissolved into the dimness of the cellar.

This was something he had never experienced. Peripheral apparitions were common in such circumstances, but he had never been subjected to an illusion that occurred in the centre of his field of vision. To counter his dizziness, he dropped to his hunkers and lowered his head. He quickly found that he could not stay in this position, he felt vulnerable, like he was offering the back of his neck to the dwarf. With a shiver of foreboding he stood up and edged his way around the room to the door.

He decided to find the others.

They were in the bar, sitting by the fire. Both of them had

a pint of dark brown Bishop's Beard in front of them on the table. He joined them.

"Cheers," said Matt, before taking a drink.

"Watch out for that stuff. It's pretty strong."

Lisbeth took a sip from her glass.

John looked at his watch and was surprised to see his hand was shaking. He dropped it out of sight. "I'm all ready to finish the job. If you guys would like to come down, we can wrap it all up before dinner."

Matt pulled a face. "Actually, mate, do you mind if we take a break? I'm feeling a bit worse for wear. I think I'd like to just chill out before going back down. How about after dinner?"

John shrugged. "Up to you. It's probably a good idea. I need to get down to the shop in the village. If it's still open. You want anything?"

They didn't. He went over to the bar where Kelly was waiting for him, smiling.

"Get a you a drink?" she asked, brightly.

"Not just now, thanks. The shop in the village, what time does it close?"

She thought for a moment. "Usually six, but seven on a Saturday."

It was just past six. He thanked her and told her that if anyone was looking for him he'd gone to the shop and would be back soon.

The night was colder than the previous one. The rain had eased but the mass of clouds suggested it would start again soon. John buttoned up his coat and hunched his shoulders against the chilly wind blowing off the sea. He made his way out of the gravelled courtyard, onto the road, and started down the incline.

As soon as he was beyond the lights of the inn, John realised just how dark it was on the country lane. He took out his phone and called home. Catherine answered.

"Hello?" she said.

"Hi, darling. It's me."

There was a few moments silence. When she spoke again it was with an inflection of mild annoyance.

"Oh, hello."

John asked how she was, how their son was. She reminded him it was the night of Maggie's party and that Brandon was at her mother's.

"Yeah, of course," he said awkwardly. "So, you off soon?"

"I'm getting ready."

"Should be a good party."

She replied, but the reception had gone and her voice was distorted, stuttering.

"Hello? Catherine . . . Can you hear me?"

There was no further response. He sighed and put the phone away. Images of Catherine in her favourite party dress danced through his mind. She was laughing, lips painted red, a devilish grin. He tried to imagine himself there with her, gathering her for an embrace, but she was skipping away, into a crowd of faceless men, beaming, flirting, careless with her attention. Despite himself, his mind's eye picked out a man's hand upon her hip, her dress discarded in a strange bedroom.

"No," he said to himself forcefully, steering his concentration to his immediate surroundings.

The high banks of the road cut off the view for most of the way. Here and there, gaps in the hedges gave him sight of the dark hillside. At a bend in the road he climbed up the embankment to see where he was going; at the bottom of the hill he could see the lights of Little Banting. He set off again, walking with long, purposeful strides and maintained a good pace. It took him twenty minutes to get to the edge of the village.

Just before the road widened to meet the main street, he crossed a stream. As he went over it, he could hear that it was gushing, a result of all the rain they'd had throughout the day. He didn't remember seeing a stream on the hillside when he had taken a walk that morning. Looking back up the hill, he tried to determine the path of the flow, but it was impossible in the dark.

The village was quiet. He saw the other shop he had noticed when passing through the night before. It was a post office, or at least it had been, it looked as though it had been closed for some years. A poster in the window, yellowing, the corners curling, advertised a long out of date saving scheme.

He continued walking. Across the street he could see the pub, the King's Head. There was light in the windows but, like the village, it too seemed deserted. The shop, Dunning's Store, was still open. He entered and a bell rang above his head.

The place was a grocers, newsagents, off licence and DVD outlet. Sweets were arranged on a stand to one side of the counter. He went over and began examining the wide array. As he did, a voice called from beyond the door behind the counter.

"I'm just coming, Josie. You're early tonight."

"Um, hello?" said John, feeling he needed to identify himself as not Josie.

The door opened and an elderly woman peeked out. "Oh. Excuse me. I took you for someone else."

She came out from behind the door and assumed a position by the till. Her hair was uniformly grey, cut in a ragged bob. She wore fine, gold-rimmed glasses and the air of someone waiting for an explanation.

"I just came down for some chocolate," said John.

"Of course, yes."

He went back to scanning the products. "Do you have any fair trade chocolate?"

"Fair trade? Sorry love. Only what you can see."

John hesitated. He eventually took a hundred gram bar of Num Num milk chocolate and the same of dark chocolate with orange flavouring. The woman rang the prices into the till.

"Three pounds, thirty-eight, please."

He took out his wallet and searched for change.

"You staying round here?" she asked as he handed over the coins.

"Yes, actually. At the Dawlish."

She dropped the coins into their respective compartments and fished out his change. "Oh, very nice. Lovely old place, it is. Wonderful food."

"Yes, certainly is." He put the chocolate into his coat pocket. "I've heard it's haunted as well."

She bit her bottom lip and glanced at the door. Then she smiled. "That's what they say."

"You've heard stories?"

"Stories, yes." She started arranging a display of locally-branded miniature surf boards that sat in a pot next to the till.

"Sorry to pry. I'm doing some work while I'm staying there. I don't suppose you could tell me something of what you've heard?"

She fixed her eyes on him, pale green eyes with tiny pupils. "I knew someone, old friend, she worked the bar. One night, she tells me, she's down in the cellar when she hears something. She turns and there's this woman all in white stood there, not three yards from her. She quit after that."

"I'm not surprised."

The woman came out from behind the counter and went to the door. "I'm closing now. So, if there's nothing else."

John shook his head and stepped out onto the pavement. The woman watched him from the doorway.

"Thanks. For the chocolate," he said, buttoning up his coat.

"I hope you're not there to stir things up."

"Excuse me?"

"People come, try to rile whatever's down there. It's not a good idea. Digging round down there. Best to leave some things alone." She turned, went inside and quickly closed the door.

For a moment he considered going to the King's Head for a quick half and an attempt to get more information on the Dawlish. He decided not to. The pub, with its meagre lighting, did not look welcoming. He set off back to the inn.

About halfway up the hill, approaching a tight bend in the road, he heard an odd noise. It got louder. He stopped to listen. The verge in front of him lit up; bare trees and high hedgerow bursting into light. John suddenly understood what was happening. He threw himself to the side of the road, pressing his body against the grassy bank as the car roared past. Over the top of the revving engine he could hear pop music, and he caught a momentary glimpse of the taxi driver, his face twisted in a manic grimace. Then the car was gone, taillights disappearing round the curve.

John picked himself up, wiped the grassy wetness from his clothes and stared after the taxi. A realisation struck him with some force: had he not jumped when he did he could have been killed. He needed a drink. To calm himself he took out the milk chocolate and ate a few squares. From far off he heard an engine being pushed to its limit. Looking south, he made out the headlights of the taxi speeding along the road to Braunton.

It began to rain. He started walking again, keeping well to the right of the road.

11.

USING A CEILING beam as the top of the frame, and the back wall to close off the right of the composition, Lisbeth set the focus of her digital SLR camera on Kelly, who was standing behind the pumps, diligently filling a pint glass with beer. The centre and left of the image took in a few of the tables and customers sitting at them, softened by lack of focus to an impressionistic blur.

Kelly's face, catching the glow of one of the ceiling spotlights, reflected and made golden by the brass plaque on the post next to her, was a study in concentration. Her blonde eyebrows bent toward each other and the tip of her tongue pressed between tightly drawn lips. Her left earring, a rectangle of greenish glass, sparkled charmingly, as did the garnet ring on the hand which held the head of the pump, gripping it as if great effort were required to pull the lever down.

Lisbeth pressed the button. The camera sounded its mimical click. She took a few more rapid snaps of the set up, then the pint glass was full and Kelly, smiling now, moved out of frame.

Having checked the photos on the camera's screen, Lisbeth lowered the instrument to her lap and took another mouthful from her own pint. She liked Bishop's Beard. It was full-bodied, nutty, with a warming, spicy aftertaste. With a smack of her lips she set down the empty glass.

"Damn, that's good stuff."

Matt was sitting next to her doing something on his phone. She nudged him. "Your round, sick boy."

He looked up at her glass, then at her. "You're going to be puking yourself if you don't slow down."

"I can drink you under the table. Remember Skegness?"

"I'd rather not." He put away the phone, finished his own drink and, taking the two empties, went to the bar.

Lisbeth snapped a few photos of him shamelessly flirting with Kelly as she pulled the pints. When she looked at them on the camera's screen, zooming in on their faces, she noticed in one image a look of malice on Kelly's face, a momentary flash of spite. Lisbeth considered it perfectly normal from a pretty girl being flirted with by a customer. The camera had caught a split second slip of pretence and it was a good picture. Despite this, Lisbeth found the image disturbing and she deleted it, telling herself it was blurred. In the next photo she noticed a sadness in Matt's eyes. Regardless of the easy smile, the confident stance, his eyes showed a wistful sentiment. Kelly, professional mask back in place, displayed a combination of detachment and coy eagerness. In the following picture, Matt had lost his poignant mien and was projecting confidence again. In response, Kelly looked less like a young woman and more like an adolescent.

When Matt returned, Lisbeth took her drink and glanced at the bar. "Would you do her?"

"What?" asked Matt, sitting down. "The barmaid?"

"Yeah."

"You know I'm a married man."

"I know you're an inveterate flirt."

He drank and shrugged, lifted a handful of peanuts from the dish on their table. "Well, she's cute."

"Knew it," said Lisbeth triumphantly.

"What about you?"

She looked again at the bar. "Could be fun. She's clearly got a nice body under all that nerviness. If she ever managed to relax. She's probably ticklish. All over."

They drank and watched Kelly, who, unable to avoid looking in their direction, reddened when she saw they were watching her. At the appearance of Susan, coming in from the dining room, the younger woman stiffened and carried on with her tasks in a brisk, proficient way.

Soon after, the Artist arrived. He entered with a booming hello, took off his coat with a flourish, and hung it by the door. From across the room he ordered a double whisky then approached the bar and leaned his back against it as he surveyed the room. His gaze lingered on Lisbeth who unabashedly returned it.

"Oh yeah?" said Matt under his breath.

"I smell a randy old goat," answered Lisbeth from behind her pint.

The Artist took his drink and said something to Kelly who immediately blushed and responded with mock offence. He downed the whisky, banged the glass on the bar and slowly wiped his mouth with the back of his hand. He then went through to the dining room from where they could hear him booming another greeting.

Halfway through their second pints, the journalists touched on what was going on in the room below. Matt wanted it to be infrasound. His own gut reaction was all the convincing he needed. It would make a great story, ages old mystery solved by modern technology. Lisbeth argued for something else.

"What though?"

She fiddled with her camera lens. "Something." She knew Matt would push, so she continued. "I don't know. Why can't there be ghosts. I mean, he's talking about sound, that's vibrations, right? Energy. It might be measurable, but that doesn't mean you can understand it."

"Does it frighten you?"

"Me? No."

He raised an eyebrow. "Not at all?"

"Just because I don't know what it is, doesn't mean I'm frightened of it."

"Would you go down there alone?"

"Fuck yeah. You daring me?" she sat back and regarded him.

"Go on, then."

She cracked a half smile, gave a curt nod and stood. "Anyway. I need some pictures of it empty." She downed her drink. "If I'm not back in ten minutes . . . bring me another pint."

Lisbeth made her way across the room. After a few words with William, who was already wobbly and responded with a half-hearted joke, she turned her attention to Kelly.

"Kelly? Hi. Lisbeth." She held up the camera. "Gotta take some snaps. John warned me to make sure you all knew if I went down."

Kelly walked over, flicked the light switches, and held the door open for her. Lisbeth thought her smile odd. Feeling condescended to, she went down the steps.

Almost immediately she came back up again. Kelly thought she would laugh out loud.

"Actually, can you turn the light off in the second room, the haunted one?"

"Off?"

"Yes. I want a long exposure."

Kelly obliged. She returned to the glasses, shaking her head.

On going back down the steps, Matt's earlier warning popped into her head. *Just don't go down alone.* She rolled her eyes. There was nothing here to be afraid of. Jittery barmaids and canny innkeepers had kept the haunting alive, feeding its smouldering legend with the oxygen of oft-repeated stories and the kindling of first-hand yarns. All her talk of there possibly being *something* down here was a wind up. She liked to play ghost's advocate simply for the sake of argument. It annoyed her when people, usually men, declared that everything could be explained away. She liked a little mystery, if only for its ornamental quality. Her entire adult life, observed through the viewfinder of a camera, had been a quest for objective truth. She had complete faith in this way of living. The truth of this particular situation was that everything untoward in the cellar was subjective; all she could do, in a professional capacity, was capture a little of the eerie appearance of the place.

She stopped at the doorway to the inner room. It was perfect now. Just enough light to give it a really spooky feel. She set up her tripod in the doorway, a low shot, angled to take in the chimney and beams, whilst avoiding the big red boiler.

As she worked, she moved around the room, centring always on the chimney. In one shot she picked up an odd reflection of light from the doorway in the dead screen of the poker machine. The result was a good one and she experimented with it.

It was irrefutable that the atmosphere in the cellar was peculiar. After only a few minutes, Lisbeth was feeling its influence. Her thoughts were becoming confused, her mind sluggish. Her skin tingled, and at a deeper level, somewhere within her body, at some point impossible for her to locate, an agitation was growing, souring her mood. It occurred to her, and she was eager to acknowledge the idea, that infrasound would be a fine explanation for what she was experiencing; invisible, yet powerfully affective.

So as to get a better sense of the flux in the room's atmosphere, she stood still and waited. Despite herself, she was feeling jumpy. Her heart was thumping and this amused her. Here was the very thing she thrived on—the buzz of nervous excitement. Even the week spent on a photo assignment in Afghanistan had been unable to produce anything as pressing as this; there had been anxious moments, but these had been the straightforward peril of random violence: roadside bombs or out of the blue mortar shells. Lisbeth had long been unfazed by the fear of being hurt. Quite early in her life she had found it necessary to learn how to manage pain, to disassociate mind from body.

What she was experiencing in the cellar was an apprehension of something intangible. This was not the panic of impending pain, this was something much deeper, and much more dangerous because of it, something nourished by anguish, capable of engendering despair. If the mind were to be wounded, there would be nowhere left to retreat.

Disquieted by these fancies, she went back to work. Down by the hearth she studied the back plate of the fireplace. From a pocket in her body warmer she took out a penknife and started scraping at the sooty surface of the cast iron plaque. There was a pattern, human figures, a tall one and short one, looking up at the other. She quickly set up the camera to photograph it, thinking that on her computer, later, she could play with the contrast and really bring out the design. As she looked through the viewfinder, the corner of her eye caught something move outside the frame.

It was very quick. She turned, reaching for the torch and knife at the same time. An undeniable intuition that she was not alone promptly crept up on her, and she felt a coolness spread from the crown of her head down to her toes. Lisbeth realised she was afraid. Ridiculous as it seemed to her, she was afraid. She stood up, heart really hammering now, all five senses on full alert, torch in one hand, penknife brandished in the other. The room tightened and she decided to get out. At all costs, she had to get out.

Then she saw it.

12.

As JOHN ENTERED the inn, he spied Matt sitting at a table near the fire. The journalist was obviously beginning to get hungry again: he had all but finished a bowl of peanuts and was on his second pint. He looked up from his phone, saw the other, and waved to him. John went and sat with him.

"Where's Lisbeth?"

"Down below."

"Alone?" John was surprised.

"She's like that. Always something to prove. Fancy a pint?"

He did. When Matt returned with two pints of Bishop's Beard, John momentarily considered taking his back. He accepted the drink, however, knocked his glass against Matt's and took a small sip.

John checked his phone and looked disappointed. He rummaged in his bag, taking out his music player and large headphones as he looked for something else.

Matt picked up the headphones. "I suppose these are quite pricey."

"Yeah. Not the most expensive, but the best suited to me."

He asked him what music player he used and John began an account of the pros and cons of digital compression. He explained the principle of lossy and lossless data encoding.

"Your average MP3 file needs to be small. Well, it used to, storage capability is increasing rapidly, but anyway, it's standard that MP3s sacrifice quality for size. To do this they cut frequencies at the top and low end of the spectrum.

Mostly you wouldn't notice it, especially when using normal speakers or earphones. All the same, you're missing a lot of what makes the music dynamic, things you're not even aware of, though they make a difference. This is lossy compression, because you're losing parts of the sound."

He went on to describe the free lossless audio codec, or FLAC, which manages to reduce the size of the end file, but limits the loss of frequencies across the range. The fact that the technology was open source and royalty free made it all the more better.

Matt tried on the headphones and was surprised by their lightness, and the effect on his hearing, even without playback. John turned on his music player and selected Steve Reich for Matt to appreciate the sound quality. The journalist nodded his head, although he admitted he couldn't really discern anything special in what he was hearing. Besides, he did not like what he considered ambient music.

He took off the headphones and looked at his phone. "Quarter past seven. I guess we can eat when Lisbeth comes up."

Just as he said this, she appeared at the door to the cellar. They immediately knew something was wrong. She didn't look in their direction as she hurried through the bar and up the stairs.

The two men turned to each other.

"I suppose I'd better go see what's up," said Matt quietly.

John waited. Despite his wariness of the drink, he finished his pint quickly. He set down the glass and as he did he noticed his left hand. It was trembling. Across his fingers the barely visible ridge of the old scar ran along three of the knuckles. He clenched his hand tight, then relaxed it. The shake was still there.

Lisbeth reappeared, Matt behind her. John was about to ask how she was when he noticed Matt signalling not to say anything.

"Shall we eat?" suggested Lisbeth with a forced smile.

The guinea fowl had been roasted in a cider baste and was served with lemon-flavoured risotto. Tiny glazed carrots and caramelised onions decorated their plates. With the meal they drank a red from the Languedoc. They ate in near silence.

All the tables in the dining room were busy. Families, couples, and two solitary diners, one of which was the hiker John had noticed that morning. From the snug they could hear the Artist laughing and carrying on with his friends. In the background, a compilation of slow movements from popular classical pieces warmly ironed out the mood of the room.

Susan, with a subtle ubiquity, presided over everything. She was at hand every time a course was finished or a bottle needed replacing; chatting amiably with the unfamiliar, gossiping in hushed tones with the regulars. Her manner with the Artist was one of playful pushiness, and they could hear his schoolboy-like replies as she chastised his coarseness and bad jokes.

When they had finished, she cleared their plates and told them she would be back with the dessert menu. Matt nipped out for a smoke. The remaining two sat in silence for a while. John filled their glasses with the last of the wine.

"I suppose you're wondering what happened," said the photographer at length.

"Something happened?"

"Yes." She drank, replaced her glass and joined her hands. "I went down to get some photos of the room with no one in it. After a few minutes I started feeling odd. Then I started seeing things. White flashes."

She straightened in her chair and fixed him with defiant eyes. "I don't scare easily. I've been to Iraq. I've been shot at by the Taliban in Helmand. But down there, in that cellar, that's the first time in a long time that I've felt real fear."

Matt came back, smelling of cigarette smoke and cold air. He sensed the mood at the table and said nothing. Lisbeth continued.

"I was over by the chimney. Facing it. I stood up and it

was like I knew, I mean I *knew* that someone was behind me. And they were a threat. I was about to turn around when I saw a man—I'm sure it was a man—he was reflected in the glass of the poker machine. He walked right by me. I saw his reflection. I know I did, and you can tell me all you want about vibrations and eyeballs, but I saw him . . . "

John noticed she was now avoiding eye contact with himself and Matt, and conjectured she was hiding something. She was very definite it was a man she had seen; he guessed that the infrasound had caused her mind to tap into deeply buried fears, perhaps a childhood trauma. It was a testament to the strength of the subsonic waves.

"So, I freaked out and ran upstairs." She laughed, stopped suddenly and picked up her glass. "I left my camera down there."

Matt was frowning at the tablecloth in front of him. "You left your camera?"

She shrugged, drained her glass. John watched with a neutral expression.

Lisbeth summoned Susan and she appeared, dessert menus in hand. She and John chose the chocolate and pear tart. Matt had pumpkin and orange cheesecake with dark rum sauce. They all had coffee.

For the rest of the time at the table, conversation revolved around city life, the merits of the countryside, and travel. Lisbeth shared some of her Afghan exploits.

After they ordered another round of Bishop's Beard, Matt steered their talk back to the subject of supernatural events. Kelly lingered when she brought the fresh pints, eager to hear some of what they said. Matt noticed and addressed her.

"Kelly, you asked us earlier what we saw, down in the cellar. What do you see?"

She wrung the cloth in her hand. She looked for Susan, then came closer. "I've never seen its face. It's always got its face covered."

The silence following this became too acute. The three visitors felt compelled to end it but struggled for something to add. It was clear from the way Lisbeth had almost turned her back to Kelly she thought the girl an attention-seeker, milking the story. Matt was staring intently at the young woman, sizing her up. His eyes lingered on her bosom and it was clear what he was thinking: country inn, virgin barmaid, midnight ravishing—a great story.

John looked at his glass and tipped the last of the ale into his mouth. He felt uncomfortable with the girl standing over them.

"But the voice is always the same," added Kelly, at last.

"It speaks?" asked John, turning.

"It says my name. Not out loud. In my head, like." She went back to the bar where the Artist and his two friends were arguing amiably as they waited to be served.

"Jesus," said Lisbeth. "I do *not* want to start hearing it."

"Liz, come on." The alcohol had blunted Matt's patience. "You know there's no ghost down there. It's sound waves, fucking with your head. I can't believe you left your camera behind."

"I don't know," she snapped. "Yes. Maybe it *is* sound waves. But what if the sound waves are a by-product. You ever think about that? What if ghosts, or spirits, or whatever, find it easier to manifest themselves when there's infrasound? Like it's a means for them, a . . . a way for them to enter our world." She directed the end of her sentence at John.

He shrugged. "I'm not arguing about what you believe; that's your choice. I see it differently."

Matt was scribbling. He pointed his pen at John.

"Differently, yeah. In your book, you talk about how you yourself perceive sound waves. Tell me some more."

He shrugged. "It's only a personal theory."

"Right, but tell me anyway." He took out his recording device and placed it on the table.

John sat back. "When I was six years old I was on holiday with my mother in Norfolk. We spent a day on the beach at Cromer. It was freezing cold, but I went for a swim anyway."

As he spoke, the familiar colours of the memory came to him: the grey of the sea, the grey of the sky, the orange and blue of his swimming trunks. He remembered how the wind caused mini sandstorms to spray against his ankles as he ran out to the low tide sea, across pebbles and slimy rocks. By the time his mother managed to get him out of the water, his lips were blue and his head was numb. That night the fever was relentless. He was taken to a local hospital and kept in for three days. His mother spoke of how she believed he was at death's door, and this image, his six-year-old self stood at an immense, black door, became intimately bound up with the confused recollections of his fevered dreams. The grey sea, the grey sky, the orange swimming trunks and the black door. His mother would tell of his screams, a result of an earache caused by infection, how he had to be isolated from the other children on the ward. He recovered, but his hearing was never the same.

"I don't know if this is medically the case," he carried on, "but the best way I can describe it is that it's like my left ear hears things a fraction of a second later than the right. We all have a difference in hearing from ear to ear, due to the distance between them. It's known as interaural time difference, and it helps us tell where a sound is coming from. Maybe this slight increase in my interaural time difference does something special. It's like I can hear in 3D."

Matt was nodding. "Great. I love it." He put away his pen, the notebook and recording device. He lifted his glass. "We should go down. Before we get wasted on this stuff."

Lisbeth agreed. They got up and walked to the end of the bar.

"Back to work, then?" quipped William as they passed.

"Time to finish it," said John, leading the way.

13.

UPON ENTERING THE inner cellar, Lisbeth went to the fireplace and recovered her camera. Matt stood by the door, unwilling to go further.

John started up the laptop. Common sound frequencies rippled onscreen, and towering above them was the immobile peak of the infrasonic wave. With the photographer following his every move, he stepped into the hearth and ducked down under the mantelpiece. The back plate, scraped clean by Lisbeth, caught his attention and he studied the image. A tall figure and a short one, holding the other's hand. He instantly thought of William.

"Matt, can you come and keep an eye on the laptop? I need to know what's happening while I'm in the chimney."

Obviously reluctant, Matt nevertheless took up position in front of the computer. John gave him a thumbs up, lifted the piece of wood and began to wedge it inside the flue. Click, click, click went the camera.

"Okay," said John, his voice swallowed by the chimney. "Any change?"

Matt bent closer to the screen.

"Matt?" said John, peering out from the hearth.

"There's . . . there's a kind of change."

Her camera lowered, Lisbeth was rubbing at her right ear. John had become immobile in the fireplace, his head cocked, listening. Matt stared at the screen, eyes out of focus, his face blank, pale and fallen. Each of them had felt the change although none of them, if asked, could have identified what exactly the change had been.

John came out from the hearth, moving slowly as if drunk. He walked to the computer to see it for himself. Matt was breathing rapidly, studying the screen intensely. Lisbeth was now shaking her head to the side, looking as if she was trying to clear water from her ear. The atmosphere in the room had seemingly thickened, had become dense with a pervasive mood of something unpleasant. They looked at one another, at once sharing the sentiment, yet unwilling to admit it.

Eventually, John managed to break the silence. His mouth was dry and his voice came out scratchy and unsure.

"That can't be right." He tapped a few keys on the laptop, frowning, his jaw hanging open. "How can it do that?"

Lisbeth lifted her camera to catch the strange look on John's face, but as she located him in the viewfinder, she hesitated. What's the point? she asked herself. Why bother with one more photograph? The great gulf of an ancient depression opened up in front of her; it widened and rebuked her, within seconds it made a mockery of all her resolutions, the late night promises made unto herself. She was fourteen again. She was in that house again, in that bed, and he, the man she knew, tall, shadowed, minatory, was in the room again. She expelled all the air from her lungs in a deep sigh that deflated her. She slumped. Her chest constricted, as if his weight was on her again, confining her, pressing against her bladder. The camera in her hands became a terrible weight; it threatened to pull her down. She wanted to put it back in the fireplace.

John was shaking his head. "I don't get it," he said feebly. The spike of the 16.9Hz sound wave had gone. In its place was another reading, a shorter spike, sharper, vicious-looking. This peak measured the presence of sound waves resonating at precisely 19Hz.

I've finally found it, said his mind.

His thoughts became bewildered as he tried in vain to

rationalise what he was seeing. The chimney was now blocked, it was not possible for it to be creating infrasound, yet the peak registered by the computer showed otherwise. Unless . . . unless the chimney's infrasound had been masking the slightly higher frequency of 19Hz, which was itself the real cause of the haunting. It was entirely possible, but if this was so, where, he asked himself, was the source of the 19Hz?

Whilst the other two were wrestling with their sudden doubts, Matt had all but lost the battle with his own. It started the moment they returned to the cellar. Despite the fact he stayed by the door, he felt his mind was being invaded by alien thoughts. Initially, he sought solace in professionalism and busied himself with his notepad, jotting down ideas as they came to him: *Years of cobwebs . . . subterranean homesick ghost . . . subsonic spirits . . . barrels and ladders and coiled ropes . . .* He struggled to find an objective frame of reference, but his notes increasingly struck him as random and disjointed. There was no cohesion, there was no logic. His faculty for correlation was deserting him and meaning, narrative, conclusion, these bedrocks of his career, indeed his mental state, were breaking up and being washed away by the relentless waves of disturbance emanating from the cellar.

He fought these feelings, battled their ferocious onslaught. With an immense effort of will he managed to stop himself running from the room. The urge to do so buffeted him, pounded him, but he stood up to it, jaw clenched, hands as fists; he resisted what every instinct in his body was telling him to do. With a weak flash of hope, Matt believed he had beaten the sensation, that he was winning. Then his stomach turned and a second later the cheesecake, the guinea fowl, the beer, the peanuts, all of it erupted from his throat in a brownish torrent and splashed onto the ground.

Part Three

The Hole

14.

FROM OFF THE sea, heavy clouds came like waves, pounding rain against the rise of the land. Cloud upon cloud, towering in maddening scale, obscured in the night sky, black giants battling above the earth.

John stood at the window of his room, wide-eyed before the spectacle. He held his mobile to his ear, listening to the muffled sounds coming from far away London.

"Are you still there?"

Catherine sighed. "Yes."

"What's wrong?"

There was music at her end, funk, and a babble of voices, laughter. Maggie's party in full swing. Catherine moved away from the noise.

"We can't talk about it like this," she said softly. "On the phone."

John pressed the phone closer to his head and put a finger in his other ear to block out the storm beyond the window. He turned to face the room.

"We'll talk when I get back. Tomorrow . . . okay?"

"We never do, though. I try, but it's like you just don't hear me."

He began a rapid defence of himself, she interrupted and he changed tack, began to promise he would listen to everything she wanted to say. She responded encouragingly but John suspected this was simply due to her being at a party and wishing to get back to it. Then there was another voice. A man's voice. She covered her phone and replied. Laughter. John couldn't help but see again that hand on her hip, the party dress discarded.

"Catherine? Hello?"

She returned to the phone. "Hello? John? I'm going to have to go."

"Who was that?" he asked, hating himself for doing so.

"Who? Oh, a friend of Maggie's. Call me tomorrow, let me know when you'll be home. We'll talk then."

"Catherine."

"I have to go. Bye."

He threw the phone onto the bed and glared at it. The room was illuminated by a flash of lightening, and his shadow sprung up for an instant on the wall, big and angry. He felt a pain in his mouth and realised he was grinding his teeth. The ache in the back tooth continued. He rubbed his jaw. With a silent curse, he decided against calling her back, picked up the phone, and pushed it into his pocket.

There was work to do. Work was the best option. He quit the room and went downstairs.

Matt was naked. His mouth was wide open, arms hung at his sides; his lean, firm body trembled. The room was dark. All of his attention was focused on the tiny bathroom window, the glass of which ran like a river. There was no sound other than the hiss of the rain, white noise against the black of the view. He was transfixed by it. After so long in the cellar, with it's inaudible but constant rumble, this high, crisp resonance was soothing.

He turned on the bath taps and the hiss of water from the showerhead calmed him further. He stepped into the water and it felt like absolution.

After the shower he lay on the bed, his earphones in and radio tuned to the static of an empty frequency, the volume loud. He lay very still and concentrated on breathing as evenly as he could.

The events played out again. John was in the chimney, Lisbeth by the chute, he was watching the computer screen. John said something, but he didn't catch it, then he felt himself get upset about something, he could not remember what it was, only that he had been greatly agitated. The following minute or so was a blank. He had no memory of vomiting; next thing he knew he was in the outer cellar, his head pressed against the door of the fridge. He could recall the coolness of the fridge against his forehead, how comforting it was.

His body, having ejected everything he had eaten, just about managed to get him up the stairs and into his room. Then another blackout of sorts and when he came to, he found himself at the bathroom window, naked.

The treachery of his stomach was not his main concern, this was easily explained by the infrasound. He didn't care that his body could betray him, it had done so before, usually after too much alcohol. What worried him were the blank spaces in his memory. The thought that his mind was now being affected by the infrasound was a terrifying development. He was horrified by the idea that what he had experienced was a precursor to some kind of mental illness. Can sound waves trigger psychosis? He guessed it was possible and this sent a shiver through his body. There was little he feared more in life than the thought of succumbing to mental illness. To go through the slow but irreversible degradation of personality and reason he had witnessed in his mother, this was the worst thing life had to offer.

Kelly couldn't believe it had happened again. She laughed. "The same guy? The one from *Prime*?"

Susan did not see the funny side. "As if I haven't got better things to do than clean up after him." She dried her hands on a towel and looked over the bar. "I've left a bucket down there. Just in case he decides to go back down."

"Where is he now?" asked William, still chuckling.

"Gone to lie down."

"And the other two?"

Susan nodded to a table by the fire where the Artist, his

two friends, and Lisbeth were deep in conversation. "The woman's over there. With the Artist. Perhaps I should warn her."

William tutted. "She's old enough to look after herself."

"Even so," added Susan. She shook her head. "As for the other one, he's back down in the cellar."

"Can't get enough of it, eh?"

Susan sighed and shook her head again. She straightened her skirt and lifted her chin. "Right. Enough of this nonsense. Time for the kitchen. I want the bins out and floor mopped. I'll take over here."

The bar was emptying. The Olivers had been and gone. Mr. James, the rambler, was off to bed. The young couple that had reserved the King's Room finished their drinks and called goodnight from the door to the stairs. Susan called back with a friendly smile. Young lovers, she said to herself, inadvertently glancing at William. His eyes were closed now, his body swaying ever so gently, righting itself with minute precision. Of all her years working in pubs, Susan had met a large number of men who could fall asleep sitting upright on a bar stool. William was an expert.

"Penny for 'em," said a loud voice that made her jump. The Artist was at the bar, four empty pint glasses set before him.

"Oh. Excuse me," she replied quickly, a hand going to her hair. "I was miles away."

"And at the same time I'm right here, in your picture frame," quoted the Artist. "Four pints of Beard, my dear."

As she pulled the pints, the Artist watched her closely and then looked over to the dozing William. He smiled at her.

"Tell me, Susan, when you were driving rally cars, how did you get all that hair into your crash helmet?"

"I wore a very big helmet."

He nodded sagely, then leant over the bar. "And when are you going to quit this place and run away with me?"

"When you win the lottery."

"Interesting lady, that Lisbeth."

"Oh really," answered Susan, flatly.

"She's been to Afghanistan. Came under fire from the Taliban."

"You don't say."

He took two of the full glasses to his table and returned for the others.

"She said she's here about the ghost. You changed your mind about publicity?"

Susan wiped the spillage from the surface of the bar. "Eleven pounds sixty, please."

He handed over a twenty. She took it, but he held on. "Well?"

"The reporters are here because the man who's with them said he could do something about it. That's all."

"Do something?"

She tugged the note from his grasp. "Do something. That's what he said. Although I'm starting to regret the whole thing."

15.

FEAR BEGETS FEAR. This was the conclusion John had come to following his research into the mechanics of the emotion.

There are two categories of fear, the rational and the irrational. The former is physical, invoked by a perceived threat to the safety of the individual—immediate risk to life or limb—and is countered by the usual fight or flight reactions. The latter is psychological and can only be overcome by conscious exercise of rational thought.

On a piece of A4 paper, John had drawn out a rough plan of the inner cellar. He was acting on an impulse to force some kind of order on the cellar, an attempt to elucidate his surroundings by means of diagrammatic representation. For the past hour he had been engaged in noting down measurements of sound waves taken throughout the room. Thirty-six so far. He was attempting to put together a sonic map of the space in the hope he could reveal the source of the 19Hz spike. The more readings he took, the more convinced he became that the chimney, or something near it, was causing the infrasound.

He read the numbers and positioned them on his map, but his mind was listless, slowed by alcohol and subsonic pressure. On his return to the cellar, he had fitted little yellow tubes of squidgy foam into his ears. The plugs helped, though they added to the sensation of submersion. All the same, the brooding vibrations penetrated his head and disturbed his balance. Their waves rang in his teeth, set his jaw clenching. They resonated in his skull, shivered his vision, tremored in his gut. Sometimes he imagined them hitting his body like a shower, raining on him, soaking him in their unremitting surge. He fancied he could feel it on his skin, little pulses of fluctuation, quavering the very essence of the air.

Regularly, his hand would reach down to his jacket pocket, slip inside, and snap off a few squares of chocolate. His mouth remained thick with sugary saliva, cloyingly coating his tongue, clogging the back of his throat. Again and again he swallowed it down, then, with the tip of his tongue, unsuccessfully tried to swab some of the gloop from his teeth, for the ache in the lower right molar was returning, only now it was not so vague, now it was a very definite toothache, located about two from the back. He tried to identify the problem with insensate fingers, blindly exploring the crenulate surfaces, probing for the cavity he was sure he would find.

The high tang of vomit still suffused the room. He struggled to ignore the pungent smell which, in collusion with the throb of the sound waves in his stomach, was building a to and fro of nausea that forced him to repeatedly take deep breaths and pinch his upper lip. It felt like seasickness, except the room was still, it was the air about him that was in motion—himself even, his cells, his molecules, battered and vibrated as if in a giant microwave oven.

Moving about the cellar, listening to it from all directions, seeing it from all angles, high and low, John was becoming sure that the room was in fact tilted toward the wall with the chimney. The floor inclined, and he imagined that if he were to place a ball on the ground, it would roll in that direction. And now that that he was convinced of the floor's slant, the contents of the cellar also seemed to be tipping; everything was leaning toward the back wall, the subterranean foundations themselves were skewed, which meant that the entire inn, ages old and tottering, was unstable. Hence the buttresses on the rear wall of the structure. He pictured himself losing his footing, rolling head over heels into the fireplace.

All the while, flickers of movement and fleeting shapes continued to signal from the extremities of his vision. Now and then they would pause on the periphery of his sight, teasing, and daring, and there were times when the peripheral flickering became so intense it was like a blizzard seen from the edges of a curtained window. But inside this blur, always close at hand, was the invisible thing that did not flit and did not flutter, the thing that seemed to follow him about the room. He refused to look at it. With all his powers of concentration, he strove to block out the feeling that it was just behind him, moving closer, then stepping back, only to approach again. Something humanoid, the void of its body bending the other hallucinations around it, as if refracting them. In spite of his determination to stay focused on the methodical analysis of the site, he had already identified this illusory presence as similar to that he had envisioned earlier: the shadowy dwarf. And there it was, whatever it was, right at his back, watching what he was doing, just tall enough to peer over his shoulder. His mind's eye clothed it in a dark outfit, ragged and torn trousers, a ripped filthy shirt hanging off an emaciated body.

Without turning, John got up and relocated to another part of the cellar. He placed the omnidirectional microphone and looked at the laptop screen, only at the screen, not to the side, or behind, just at the screen where the familiar pattern of infrasound was unchanging. It reassured him. The thing noticed. It had moved with him. It was now between him and the barrels. Despite himself he listened. It was breathing, close to his ear, soft and rasping, or was it whispering? Were those words he half heard? A sinister, sibilant stream of incoherent maledictions, infandous wishes directed against him. He felt faint, as though whatever was behind him was winning—it was pushing him, pushing him toward the chimney. His knuckles whitened as his fingers tried to grip the floor, his fingernails scratched the dirty tiles. In desperation he refocused his attention on the computer screen, but now the peaks and troughs of the sound waves appeared ghastly to him. The rippling jagged line of the day-to-day sounds was no longer that of the fridges, the pumps, the boiler, but an image of the voice he pretended he couldn't hear, rippling there onscreen, mocking his pretence of scientific detachment. The long, thin spike stretching above, green at the base, red-tipped, was no more the recognizable representation of a 19Hz standing wave, but a long, thin dagger, exactly like that in the stubby hand of the dwarfish creature at his back.

John gave in. He turned. The movement flickered out of sight. The voice stopped.

He waited. It started again. The whisper, to his left now, creeping nearer. Yes, it seemed to hiss, I know you can hear me.

Cursing loudly, he stood up too quickly and dizziness piled upon dizziness, and he was forced to reach out a hand to the barrels until the larger waves of disequilibria had passed. Without wanting to, he thought of his office at home, the calm, chastened air of his retreat; his body ached for it, and his heart sank further into its wounded self. He took out his earplugs and reeled again from the abrupt clarity of his hearing. I will write a paper on this one, he thought, looking again at the chimney. He walked over to it, searched around it, but there was nothing. Taking a few steps back, his eyes were drawn to the poker machine.

No, he thought approaching, it's not possible. It had just then occurred to him that the machine was perhaps plugged in and, although turned off, was creating a deep humming noise.

He pushed his upper body between the chimney and the poker machine, looking for the power lead. It was there. Reaching with his left hand he tried to take hold, but it was beyond his grasp. He needed to move the whole thing. By pushing it from the top, he managed to tip the machine a few inches, but it was far too heavy to move on his own.

John hurried from the cellar and headed upstairs.

16.

SINCE HER EXPERIENCE in the cellar, Lisbeth had been hankering for a chance to let go. The steady intake of alcohol was gradually shifting her mind away from the dread and its attendant memories. Her drinking companions were amiable enough, the Artist and his two friends were delighted to have her company and, despite the occasional innuendo, kept their dallying at an acceptable level. That said, as the evening progressed, the jokes became more ribald, the glances more disposed to linger. The Artist was archetypal: leather jacket, receding hair pulled tight in a grey ponytail, a taste for single malt chasers and sudden bursts of poetry. Another few pints and her curiousity about his "little cottage clinging to the rocks" might be excuse enough to allow him to take her home. Once there, the familiarity she considered granting him would easily conjuror up the contempt she needed to battle her personal demon.

He was in mid anecdote—an encounter with a starry sky in the Sahara—when she spotted John coming from behind the bar. He lurked like a lanky teenager building up the courage to ask for a dance.

It was after midnight and, other than her table, the bar was empty. John beckoned to her. She hesitated, then lifted her camera, excused herself, and joined him.

"I need your help," he said in a hurried whisper.

She followed him down. He pointed to the poker machine and told her it had to be moved. She looked it over.

"Right," she said, and rolled up her sleeves.

With the two of them, pushing and pulling, they were able

to tilt it, twist it, and make it step out from the corner and off the pallet. John quickly looked behind. He stretched, took hold of the power lead, and lifted it out. It was not plugged in.

Then he saw the wall. The stone he had noticed earlier, the cut stone, curved and rounded, there were others like it.

"OK," he said, standing up again, "we need to get this right out of the way."

"Seriously?" Lisbeth was red-raced from the exertion. She stepped back and, in one quick motion, pulled off her fleece. John noticed the thinness of her undershirt, the fact she wore no bra. He tried not to stare.

They took up their positions and, after a count of three, began rocking the poker machine. John felt that they were struggling uphill, that the building, with its slant toward the chimney, was purposefully making the task more difficult. Repeating the stepping process, grunting and swearing, they succeeded in shifting it all the way to the centre of the room.

With the machine gone from the corner, the force of the infrasound had gone up another few notches. The pressure on the eardrum was like that in a descending airplane. John tried to pop his ears by inducing a yawn but nothing worked.

He could see that Lisbeth felt it too. Her drunkenness cowered and slipped away. She had become chilled and quickly put her fleece back on. She wrapped her arms about herself, shivered and began mumbling.

"I think I need a big drink of water. And bed . . . My own bed. Alone."

Breathing heavily, John went back to the corner from where the machine had come. Yes, it was clear now, there was an arch in the wall. It had been filled in a long time ago, but the curvature was plain to see; at some point there had been an entry in the wall. A low one, no higher from the current floor level than about three feet.

"What is it?" asked Lisbeth, from behind her camera.

"Looks like a very old doorway. Obviously the ground

level used to be a lot lower." He lifted the pallet and stood it against the fireplace, then knelt in front of the arch, his hands running over the cold stone. That was when he noticed the floor.

"Hang on."

"What?" asked Lisbeth, approaching cautiously.

"Jesus!" He scrabbled backward, alarmed. Lisbeth also jumped back. "What? What is it?"

Creeping forward, he took out a torch. By its light they could see there was a grill on the floor and that it covered an opening. It was about the size of a manhole cover, square, gnawed by rust, but intact. The mesh was quite wide. Beneath it they caught faint glimpses of smooth stone walls surrounding a drop into total darkness. Leaning over, John could feel the force of the sound waves intensifying. The toothache became piercing, no longer an indeterminate throbbing, but a very definite, localised pain.

"It's a souterrain of some kind."

He got up again, smiling excitedly, wired by the toothache and the chase.

"A what?"

"A hole. A well or shaft, or something. And it's where the infrasound is coming from." He ran from the cellar and came back a moment later with a broom. Carefully, he brushed the area around the grill. Clearing away the last of the grime he noticed the lock. The grill was bolted shut and padlocked.

He knelt down and inspected the lock; it was an old one.

"I wonder where it leads," he said, trying to see within.

It took a long time for Matt to decide to show his face again. To hide now would only delay and add to his embarrassment.

Susan was nowhere to be seen. Most of the lights in the bar were now unlit and the last clients were gathered by the door. The Artist was there, putting on a wide-brimmed hat and casting glances to behind the bar. His friends left and he reluctantly went with them.

Kelly glanced up from the dishwasher and gave Matt a pitying look. He went over to the bar and stood next to William.

"Something you ate?" said the old man, dryly.

"What? Oh, right. Yeah, it's pretty intense down there."

"Don't worry about it. I've seen it happen before."

Matt couldn't tell if he was joking. "What about you, William? How do you deal with it?"

"Ah," he said. "Me and *it* have come to an agreement. I don't hang around down there and *it* doesn't come looking for me."

"Looking for you?"

William blinked slowly. His left hand reached for his pint, but it was gone. His face registered surprise for a moment, then he frowned along the bar at Kelly.

"Yes. Looking for me. That's a Susanism. She says it follows her around. But she's a skittery woman. As for Kelly," he turned his tiny eyes back to the barmaid, "it's the goose that says boo to her."

From where he stood, Matt could see that the cellar door was open. The other two were down there. He knew he would have to join them, but his disinclination kept him at the bar. He tried to find something to say to William, an excuse to stay where he was for a few more minutes. Nothing came. Seconds went by, agonisingly slow. He didn't want to speak to William, he didn't want a drink, yet he remained where he was, one hand resting on top of the bar, the other clenched in his pocket.

"Your friends are downstairs," said William at last. Now there was no choice but to join them.

"Yes," he said, forcing himself to move. "I'm just on my way to see them."

With heavy trepidation and his gut tying itself in knots, Matt went behind the bar and approached the door. He looked down the steps. It was quiet below. Maybe, he thought, they're not down there.

"They *are* down there," called William.

Matt went down. He stopped at the threshold to the inner cellar and carefully leant his head in to see what was happening. The poker machine was in the middle of the floor and they were in the corner it had come from, their attention fixed on the ground there.

"What's going on?"

Lisbeth jumped at the sound of his voice. "Fuck, Matt. Don't do that!"

"We found something," said John without looking up. "Come and see."

"I don't think I dare. What is it?"

He described the grill and the drop beneath it. Cautiously, Matt entered the cellar and stood over them.

"It's locked," said Lisbeth. "There must be a key nearby."

They began to search. Matt went back to the doorway.

"Of course," said John, breathlessly, and hurried to the mantelpiece. The key was still there. He snatched it up, ran to the corner and dropped to his knees. The key slipped into the padlock. He turned it and the padlock clicked open. Lisbeth and John glanced at each other, then he took out the lock and slid back the bolt.

Forgetting his wariness, Matt was drawn into the room. He slowly approached them and bent down to see. John had taken hold of the handle next to the bolt and pulled. With a creak, the grill moved a little. He let it down again.

"It's heavy," he gasped.

Matt moved to his side and took hold of a bar. He could sense the sound waves coming up from the hole, rising like vapours from a diabolical vat. It was stronger now, much stronger. He held his breath. They strained and swung the grill slowly upright.

Without a word, the three of them peered into the dim opening. John pointed his torch inside and they saw that the walls of the hole were bare, jagged stone, that the whole thing looked like a messy fracture in the bedrock. About five feet below floor level began a very narrow set of irregular steps that led down into darkness. The sight of this further descent chilled each of them.

John knew he had to go in, and now the tilt of the cellar made sense, it wasn't the chimney all things were sliding to, it was the hole in the ground. Pointing the torch with his left hand, he took out his phone and reached it as far into the hole as possible, angling it to take a photo. The phone clicked and he turned it for another view. He was just thinking he had better not drop the phone when, as he positioned his thumb for another photo, he dropped the phone. With a gasp he watched it fall from his hand into the dark. He heard a low clack, the sound of plastic hitting rock, then silence.

"Fuck," he whispered, and slumped against the wall to his right. All those photos of Brandon, of Catherine, of the three of them, smiling, together, they were all lost. The numbers and contacts, addresses and links, these were nothing, it was his family he had let slip into the hole, his last connection to them. He closed his eyes and let his head drop.

Lisbeth watched with concern showing on her face. She was in the process of reaching out to him when something made her stop. She turned slowly, then froze.

"Oh," she said faintly. The others turned and looked toward the door.

William was in the room with them.

Something about him had changed. He stood by the poker machine, tall and daunting, no longer slouching, no longer unsteady. His small eyes seemed to glow in the dull light of the cellar. His face had taken on a solemn demeanour, one which gave his long nose and tight-lipped mouth a cruel aspect.

"William," said John in surprise, sitting up. When he didn't respond, John went on. "Why didn't you tell me about this?"

He slowly closed his eyes and opened them again. "You never asked."

John would have laughed, but the way William was regarding him dissuaded it.

"What's down there?"

Taking a few slow steps back and then to the left, William began to circle the room, keeping as much distance between himself and the hole as possible. He stopped by the barrel chute. "Don't you know?"

"Obviously not," said Lisbeth. She half-raised her camera, putting it between herself and this suddenly unpleasant man, a defence mechanism. Her eyes darted to the doorway, calculating the speed of a getaway if needed.

"What's down there?" asked John again, a hardness creeping into his voice.

"Death," said William bluntly.

Matt shrunk away from the hole. His body language suggested he was beginning to populate the darkness beneath him with absurd and awful things. As soon as he had seen William in the cellar, he began glancing nervously at the door, taken by the horrible idea that the old man was planning to push him in. Like Lisbeth, he too was scheming his escape.

"Death?" repeated John with what he hoped would sound like scepticism, but which came out in an oddly high-pitched way.

"I won't stop you. If you want to go down there," William went on, now reaching the fireplace and pausing. "But I'm not responsible for whatever happens if you do. For any of you."

"Why do you say death is down there?" John was trying to take charge of the situation, he was fumbling for his scientific detachment.

"I know you can feel it," said William. "Whatever your computers and gadgets might say, I know that you, personally, can feel the power that comes from down there."

He shut his mouth firmly and stared. John returned the gaze. Everyone waited in the almost silence. The boiler clicked and rumbled, the pumps hummed, and the soundless racket from the hole poured into the already flooded room.

"I *am* going down there," said John at last, slowly and deliberately. "And I'll use one of those ropes, if you don't mind."

William put up his hands to show that it was no longer his concern. Following the same wide path, he made his way from the cellar. The other three watched him go. At the doorway he turned.

"Not responsible. For any of you." Then he was gone.

Having waited until the sound of his steps had diminished, Lisbeth shook her head. "What a nut job."

Matt was back by the doorway. "You're not seriously thinking of going down there, John."

"Of course I am."

Matt retreated a little further.

Lisbeth took a small digital camera from a pocket and handed it to John. "Take as many pictures as you can," she told him.

Together they inspected the ropes. They chose the longest and uncoiled it. Lisbeth slung the rope over the large hook above the barrel chute, tested its strength, then wound the end around her waist. She went to stand with Matt. John was reassured to see she had used ropes before. He tied a loop in the other end and fitted it over his shoulder and around his waist. He slipped his torch into his pocket and sat at the edge of the hole.

"Well. Here goes," He gave a nod. Lisbeth and Matt took up the slack. Placing his hands on the edge of the opening, he lowered himself inside.

17.

FEAR BEGETS FEAR.

Once fear is stimulated, the brain will fight to maintain control, because loss of self-control, the disintegration of personality, is the ultimate horror. The more the brain struggles to stay in command, the greater its anxiety, thus a feedback loop is created, which, if not broken, will allow the subconscious to rear up and devour the conscious mind. There will no longer be a distinction between reality and imagination, and a total collapse of the psyche will occur.

As he was lowered into the hole, John was well aware that he was experiencing both categories of fear simultaneously: the rational and irrational. The former aspect was altogether warranted, considering his situation, and he offset it by reassuring himself of his ability, if necessary, to haul himself out of harm's way. The tightness of the rope around his body was a comforting reminder that the other two were still in place above him, holding firm. As for the other kind of fear, the psychological, irrational variety, a constant recognition of its inherent absurdity was the only means to allay it. And so, the deeper he went, the more forcefully he repeated to himself that there was, somewhere in the darkness below him, a logical explanation for all the weirdness he and the others had experienced. He could sense the waves of infrasound in every part of his body, and he clung to this perception as tightly as his left hand held the rope that supported him.

Fear begets fear.

To divert his troubled mind, John summoned up the little

he knew of what was going on inside his head. The amygdala are two almond-shaped ganglion located at the front of the temporal lobe. When fear stimuli arrive, the amygdala cause the secretion of hormones, notably epinephrine and cortisol, which regulate heart rate and blood sugar levels, key elements in preparation for fight or flight. When the danger has passed, the amygdala, in conjunction with the hippocampus, plays a part in constructing a memory of the scare to be used as a reference of how to react in future situations of a similar nature. It is the stimulation of the hippocampus that causes a greater quantity of information to be memorised than usual. Later, when recalling the event, the clarity and amount of detail remembered results in the perception that time slows down during a fright.

It took no more than three or four seconds for John's descent to bring his feet into contact with the first of the steps below. In that time he scanned the walls of the fissure, wondering how many of these sensory inputs he would be able to recollect: the roughness of the shadowy rock face, its coldness against his fingertips as he steadied himself, the wetness of the stone, the smell of damp, dark, secret places long hidden from view. From the depths below a chill emanated, causing him to shiver.

With both feet on the first step, he transferred his weight to his legs and called out for some slack. He took out the torch and, one step at a time, made his way further into the hole. There wasn't much to see. The uneven walls gave way here and there to stonework, large blocks of the same creamy-grey limestone, knobbled to fill in the gaps in the rock. Pointing the torch in the direction he was going, he saw only more steps, more rock.

John heard Lisbeth's voice as if from a great distance. "John! We're running out of rope."

He looked upward and was struck by how far he had come. The mouth of the hole appeared remote and peculiar, a small rectangle of weak light surrounded by an expanse of blackness.

He shouted upward. "Take the rope off the hook and stand by the hole."

When they had complied, he started down again. He was counting the steps. After nine, he reached a level area. It was a small chamber, about five feet square. His phone lay face down on the rock floor. He picked it up. The screen was cracked. When he tried to turn it on there was no response. With a pang of anxiety he realised he could no longer call home. Then it struck him, he couldn't call anyone. He ignored the feeling and slipped the useless thing into his pocket.

With a sweep of the torch he looked around. On his right there was a gap in the rock, low and not very wide. Three iron bars had been cemented into place so as to block the way. He ducked down and shone the torch inside. A passageway led downward with quite a pronounced gradient. Just beyond the bars he could see the remains of some flowers, rotted and disintegrated in the dampness.

"I've found a tunnel," he called back to the top. "It's been closed off."

He grabbed the middle bar and tested it. Solid. The one on the left moved a little when he pulled it. Looking closely, he saw that the cement at the top was crumbling. He took out his penknife and dug at it. The cement was old and damp and came away in little showers of sand. When he tried the bar again, it came right out. The space between the middle bar and the wall was just big enough to allow him to pass. He shouted to the top that he was going into the tunnel.

Lisbeth yelled back for him to be careful. As he was about to enter, his torch picked out some markings on a smooth bit of rock above the entrance to the tunnel.

G.H.—1775—R.I.P.

The letters had been neatly carved. Next to them was a glyph he did not recognise. Below this message were more letters. *W.F.* Again those initials. Under this was another, more modern-looking bit of writing, scratched rather than engraved: *Danger!*

He pulled out the camera and took photos of the writing.

Squeezing through the gap between the wall and the central bar, he entered the passageway. The floor was a sheet of rock, wet and slippery. It sloped downward for about eight feet then levelled out. The only way he could progress was to turn and enter feet first; he could feel the cold moisture numbing his fingers, soaking into his trousers. All the while, the thick torrent of sound beat against him, except that now he fancied he could actually hear it, a gloomy buzz like a poor sound system, playing nothing, but turned to full volume. His head throbbed. The toothache was getting worse by the minute, causing him to suck at the offending tooth and rub his jaw. He stopped to fit his ear plugs but became so disorientated he immediately took them out. With a fierce determination, he tried not to think about the chambered tomb in Ireland, the cramped passageway, the tonnage of stones above him. But the vibrations were insistent, pressing at his temples to make him recall those feelings, the way it had started as a tickle of discomfort and, in moments, had become a spate of gushing panic.

He stopped and shook his head and ordered himself to get a grip.

As he descended, the volume magnified. Now he really could hear it. Whatever it was, it was big. It hissed at a high frequency, but the bass notes were also audible now, just breaking the surface of the range of hearing. He let himself slip a little farther down and found himself being pulled back. He took hold of the rope and tugged. It tugged back.

He pulled again, but had no idea what message he was sending. He called to them. No answer.

Scrambling back to the top of the slope, he called again. He was surprised to find that, even though he had reached the entrance with the bars, he could still hear the boom of the bass notes, as if it had followed him. His voice was lost in this flood of barely audible sound. It was only when he had squeezed back through the gap of the missing bar that Lisbeth finally heard him.

"What's down there?" she called.

"I don't know. There's a tunnel. I can't see where it goes."

Matt's pallid face appeared in the small rectangle of light from the cellar above. "We're out of rope."

"Damn. Well, come down here."

"I'm not going down there," said Matt. "I can barely be in this room."

"Lisbeth."

She shook her head and looked away as if shamed.

"Damn." He started to undo the knot. His fingers felt numb, and what with the trembling of his hands it took him some time to free himself from the rope.

Despite their attempts to make him stop, he went back down the tunnel. Going slowly, fingers trying to grip the smooth, wet stone, he felt the noise rising. Now, the sound was filling in the gaps between the high-toned hissing and bass notes; the rising treble brought volume. By the time the floor levelled out, it was like standing near a passenger jet just off the runway. His legs had gone weak and it was an effort to stay upright. He tried to see ahead. The paltry cone of torchlight vanished in front of him. One moment it was pointing at the hewn wall, the next, there was nothing. He peered, but the void confused his eyes.

With tiny steps, he advanced. The walls of the tunnel opened out into a wide and obscure space. Although he could not see, John could sense from the dynamics of the noise that the area in front of him was immense. He was standing before a cavern, on a ledge about two feet wide. Realising this, he pressed himself against the wall behind him. Looking down, he saw that the ledge continued to the right, tapering as it went.

Despite the fact that the sound was reverberating all

around, amplified by the echoey vastness of the cave, John knew the source was to the right. In his mind, he quickly replayed the path to this spot and concluded he was somewhere under the garden. He didn't want to go on, but he had to go on. No matter how hazardous, he had to dispel the mystery. He had to find the source.

Edging very slowly, he followed the walkway. The sound was becoming familiar, now that the full range of its frequencies was perceptible, yet he still could not identify it.

Next to him, on the wall, he saw more carvings. He shone his torch across them. These inscriptions suggested a far greater antiquity than those at the mouth of the tunnel. Crudely executed, they were nevertheless deeply incised. A line of human figures crowded together on what appeared to be a representation of the exact place he himself stood. Each of them held aloft a sword, yet these swords, in an improbable cascade, rose above them and arched downward into what looked like a pit. The hole, which he took to be drop in front of him, was drawn as two lines that became fainter as they descended, eventually petering out, perhaps implying the plunge was bottomless. The swords rained down into the pit.

He considered the petroglyph. Was it showing an attack? Was the trajectory of the swords an attempt to illustrate a battle against the pit itself? Or was it indicative of the prehistoric practice of offering swords and other metal objects to sacred places?

No sooner had he thought this than he understood what the noise was.

He moved a little further to the right, so as to confirm his theory. By now, the ledge was just a little wider than his shoes. Arms spread out either side, his hands tried to gain purchase on the wet rock; his fingers sought out tiny cracks and indents in the surface.

Yes, he thought, his head tilted toward the sound, I know what it is. Water. The resonance was that of vast quantities of water falling from a great height into a pool. It was a waterfall, the plummet of a subterranean river. This explained the booming infrasound, the power of it. All of a sudden his analytical mind was trying to imagine the size of the waterfall, it faltered and shrank back from the terrible dimensions.

Far below, the dark water churned and pummelled the air, a sinister, noisy chaos. By now the infrasound had completely stupefied him. The dizziness that had been encroaching on his consciousness all evening was winning out. His legs were feeble, aching and trembling and barely able to support him. Gazing into the black abyss, he fancied he could see shapes teeming in the air. All manner of images appeared, faint outlines of human forms, writhing and drifting, passing before his sight like floaters on the eyeball. And always, right in the middle of these imagined phantasms, the same figure that had haunted him in the cellar, the dwarf, superimposed on all the other hallucinations, untroubled when he blinked, insistent in its proximity. He stared at it, unabashed, disbelieving, yet wary, and he saw that it was not a dwarf, it was a child—a pitiful, lost and lonely child.

He felt a pull, a powerful draw from the child, as if it were exerting an awful attraction, like a black hole sucking in light. He raised the torch but it was useless. Without thinking, he lightly tossed it out in front of himself, hoping he would catch a better glimpse. It fell away and out of view.

It was only a mild surprise when he found himself in total darkness. Imprecise impressions of the plummet in front of him swirled in his head. He saw again in his mind's eye the way the swords leapt from the hands of the men and were swallowed by the pit. He asked himself if he had really thrown his torch, or if it had jumped by itself, commanded by the depths before him. Quite independent of his conscious thoughts, an idea was forming, stirred by the maddening, unknowable proportions of his surroundings. He should let himself fall. Simply throw himself into the nothingness. It would be perfect, just to let go, to follow his torch and fall forever and ever through the black and empty oblivion, his mind disintegrated, his soul dispersed. If nothing else, it would bring an end to the agony of his toothache, which by now was drowning out even the roar of the water.

"I've finally found it," he said aloud without realising.

John felt his body straighten. His back came away from the wall behind him. His hands gave up their effort to cling to the rock. He swayed, rocking slightly from the heels to the balls of his feet.

It all made sense now, the fact that his whole life was a progression to this place, to this endless end which pleasingly beckoned. As if looking at someone else's life, he thought briefly of Catherine, of Brandon. They would understand this act: He had gone down a hole and never come back. He is happy now, they would say to each other, to friends and family. He finally found what he was looking for and embraced it.

The sway of his body became more pronounced. He didn't even have to apply any effort, the magnetism of the void had taken over, pulsing him back and forth. Any second now the balance would tip and he would be released forward and forever downward.

"John," said a voice. A pleasant voice. It didn't shout, it didn't command, it simply said his name.

"Yes," he answered, smiling.

"Here I am," it offered. He looked into the cavern but saw nothing. "Here."

Turning to his left he saw a weak pool of light and within it a face he knew he should recognise. A hand reached out. That's nice, he thought, he has come for me.

The hand took hold of his arm, tightly. He looked down at it. The hand exerted some strength; it was pulling in the opposite direction. For a moment he found himself in an odd equilibrium, then the hand won out and he was forced to take a step toward the face.

"That's it," coaxed the voice.

He took another step and became conscious enough to realise he was going away from the source of the sound, away from the void. He resisted, but the hand was resolute. A sob escaped his mouth.

"This way," said the voice, "this way."

A second later, with an abrupt violence, the hand yanked him hard. He lost his balance and, following a brief moment of lucidity, shot through with regret, he fell into unfathomable depths.

18.

THE ROOM WAS a cave, or the cave was a room, he couldn't tell which. The flicker of flames from the torches made the uneven walls appear in motion. He tried to sit up, but something kept him lying on his back, a force he could not understand. Straining his head he could see that he was naked. The people crowding around him were unfamiliar, dressed in unusual clothes, long flowing robes covered in peculiar patterns. They regarded him with a uniform emotion: contempt.

William was there. "John," he said.

The press of people parted and someone walked toward him. It was Kelly. She looked younger than she was, child-like in the over-sized gown that trailed on the floor and hid her hands in its voluminous sleeves. She glared at him as she came. Again he tried to move, but his entire body was fixed.

"Kelly," he rasped. "What's going on?"

She ignored him, stood over him, and slowly bent her head toward his. He knew what she was doing, but it was still a shock. She was kissing him. Her lips parted his lips and her tongue caressed his tongue. It was a long, deep kiss. It was like his very first kiss, wonderful and terrible at the same time, embarrassing and sensual.

She straightened and stood to the left. Someone else was approaching. It was Susan. She too was dressed in robes. Her hair was wild and spread out like a primitive headdress. She too regarded him with a look that suggested madness, or fervent will, or inevitability. She stopped before him.

"John," said William.

"What's going on? Why are you—" His words were

smothered by her mouth as she too administered a deep kiss. When it broke, she rose and stepped to the right.

Now, most terrible of all, came Lisbeth. Her robes were open, her body naked beneath. On her head she wore a crown of white feathers, topped with the graceful neck and head of a swan.

"Lisbeth. Not you. What are you doing?"

When she stood over him, she too silenced him with a kiss. He yielded. He gave up struggling. He felt his body go limp. Her kiss went on and on, as she sucked at his tongue, probing his mouth with her own.

At last she broke and straightened. The crowd was intoning something, a low rumble of arcane words which he knew immediately to be an imitation of the subterranean waterfall.

Lisbeth raised her hands. Clasped between them was a dagger. A long thin dagger, green and red-tipped.

"John," said William.

She with the knife was chanting something, her voice rising, becoming shrill, passing right out of his range of hearing.

The dagger came down.

19.

"JOHN."

On opening his eyes, he found himself in a house he did not recognise. He lay on a black leather sofa. A widescreen television faced him, behind it a wall of books; cream curtains draped the window, and a tall, modern lamp cast a circle of white light on the ceiling.

"Welcome back," said William.

Sitting up, John felt like he was coming round from a general anaesthetic. Unfortunately, the ache in his tooth was waking up as well. "Where am I?"

"How's your head?"

"What happened? Where am I?"

William was pouring something. For a horrible few moments, John was convinced it was more ale. It was water.

"Drink."

He didn't realise how thirsty he was until he finished the glass. He held it out for more and drank again.

William sat on the chair next to the sofa. There was a new element to his face, an unfamiliar arrangement of the lines about his forehead. It was a frown, but not that of the old man against the world which normally shaped his brow, this was a deeper, more authentic expression. It spoke of someone who had grappled with a great pain over many years, the outward manifestation of a deep-seated anguish. On seeing it, John felt obliged to hold off his questions and wait.

William sighed. His small, deep-set eyes were fixed on the base of the sofa but they had lost focus. The man was looking elsewhere.

"When I was eight years old my father bought The Dawlish and we moved here from Weymouth."

He spoke softly, in monotone, it was the sound of someone trying to manage great emotions.

"There were five of us. Father, mother, my older sister, myself and my younger brother. Daniel. He was six . . . My father did not believe in ghosts, but he did believe in dangerous holes in the ground. He padlocked the grill in the cellar and my brother and I were forbidden from going anywhere near it."

He looked up, suddenly back in the room. "Do you have children, John?"

"A five-year-old boy. Brandon."

"Then you will know that to forbid a child from doing something is to invite them to do it . . . " His line of sight slid down again as he lowered his head.

"I knew where the keys were kept. I knew which key I needed. One afternoon I took the key and opened the padlock. I was terrified, I was determined, but there was no way I was going down that hole on my own. Daniel was easily persuaded; he was obsessed with pirates so I told him there was treasure under the cellar. We used a ladder to get down to the steps. I had an Eveready torch, silver body, blue around the handle, a beautiful thing . . . "

He shifted in his seat and his head tilted, but his eyes, glaring once again at a point at the base of the sofa, did not move.

"I went first. I was so frightened. So very frightened. It felt as though something was trying to push me, to stop me from going on, but with Daniel behind me, I couldn't back down. I kept on going, down the tunnel, right to the edge . . . I stopped there, couldn't see a thing, even with the torch. Daniel, though, he wanted his treasure. He pushed past me, kept going."

The tears came all of a sudden, streaking down his cheeks and gathering at his chin to drip between his legs to the parquet floor.

"I remember him in the torchlight, the brightness of his green jumper in all that blackness, I told him to stop . . . one second he was there, the next he was gone . . . I called and I called and I called. Nothing. I left the grill open and hid in my room."

At long last he lifted his eyes and looked at John. "When it was clear Daniel was missing, my father found the open grill and guessed what had happened. He confronted me and I told him everything. After the enquiry, my father sold the inn. Daniel's body was never found. We moved to London. Never told anyone. I ended up following in my dad's footsteps and became a landlord."

William stood up and got himself a glass. When he came back his face was dry.

"Susan and I came down here five years ago, an anonymous visit. I saw the place for sale . . . I guess it was an act of attrition. Susan's word. She's the only person I've ever told. When we moved in, I went down there, saw the bars my father put in to block the way. Every year, on Daniel's birthday, I go down and leave some flowers." He shrugged. "Makes me feel a bit better."

He was quiet after this. John, unwilling to break the silence, waited. After some minutes he felt he should say something.

"You still blame yourself?"

"What? Blame myself? Of course I do. I'll always blame myself. But it's easier now."

"Your initials. I saw WF, but I thought your name was Colson."

"That's Susan's name. She kept it when we married. My name is Finch. William Finch. We bought the Dawlish in her name. I didn't want anyone remembering my family. Daniel's disappearance. And I insist you keep this story to yourself. It mustn't go any further."

John nodded. He took a deep breath and sighed. He was feeling very tired. The ache in his tooth had abated but was still painful. Without thinking, he moved his tongue across the cavity.

William began to speak again. "You asked me two things, what happened and where are you. Well, this is our flat, it's built on top of the kitchen. As to what happened, I can't really say. The other two told me you'd gone in, and I found you on the edge of the drop, in total darkness. You looked like you were about to jump. To be honest, I'm in no doubt I saved your life. I lost one life down there, now I've saved one. I think the cellar and I are equal. Perhaps now I can let go."

John closed his eyes at the memory. He shivered as he recalled those last few moments before he passed out. "I was . . . I don't know, hypnotised. Some kind of trance brought on by the noise down there."

"That's one way of putting it."

"How would you put it?"

"I wouldn't. Some things need time before you talk about them. Now, if you're feeling better, we'll go see the others. They're very worried."

William followed him to the stairs and insisted again that the secret be kept, then he bade him goodnight. Lisbeth and Matt were waiting in the bar. They stood when John walked in. He assured them he was fine, and in response to his questions, they told him that William had managed to drag him to the mouth of the tunnel and that from there the three of them got him out of the hole and up to the flat. Lisbeth related how she had been adamant that an ambulance be called, and how William had refused. He told them John would be fine, that he needed to discuss something with him when he woke up.

Again and again they asked him what exactly took place down there. He told them about the cavern, about the underground river being the origin of the infrasound, that he had passed out due to the noise, that William found him and got him out, had, in fact, saved his life.

"And what did William want to discuss?" asked Matt.

John yawned deeply and his ears popped for the second time since he had come round. "William told me," and he yawned again, "William told me that a very close friend of his died down there, and he felt responsible. That's why he hid the entrance. He doesn't want it out in the public again."

"Well, look, I'm here for a story, and I'm going to—"

"You can write your story, but none of that goes in. I found a subterranean river, that's what's causing it all."

The reporter shrugged. "We'll talk about this later."

Having been assailed by waves of adrenaline for the past few hours, John felt wide awake, though when he had showered and gently brushed his teeth, taken two painkillers and lain down in bed, he fell fast asleep.

20.

HE WAS THE last to get up, finally surfacing around eleven. The kitchen was closed, nevertheless, Susan provided him with toast and scrambled eggs. He felt as though he had spent the previous night at a rave: His ears were ringing, his mind was woolly and slow, and his body ached as though he had run a marathon. His sleep had been dreamless and deep. He drank a lot of coffee.

Susan busied herself clearing the dining room. On asking after the others, he was told Lisbeth and Matt had gone for a walk.

John took out his phone and showed Susan the cracked screen. "I need to call my wife . . . "

She told him he could make the call from her office.

The room smelt of cigarette smoke and lemon air freshener. He sat at the desk and dialled. In front of him, written in neat script under the heading Saturday, was Susan's to do list: *contact Devon Tourist Board, pick up the new saucepans, call Marjorie, order more cards for—*

"Hello?"

Catherine's voice cut straight to the heart of John. He felt himself tense.

"It's me."

"Hi," she said weakly.

"How are you?"

He heard her take a deep breath. "A little hung over. Maggie had us all drinking rum . . . and you?"

John wondered how he was. He imagined adding to the to do list—*find out how I feel.* There was a blankness inside, an empty space, hollowed out to make room for a new set of values. Just what those values would be he as yet had no idea. At that moment, what concerned him most was the need for an immediate and conclusive reconnection with the woman on the other end of the line. To achieve this meant the complete abrogation of all suspicion about what had happened the previous evening at Maggie's party, and after. The party dress removed from the floor and neatly hanging in the wardrobe.

"I'm—I had a hell of a night."

Shall I tell her, he asked himself, that I almost died? That last night I went to the limits of my world and very nearly stepped off the edge. That I am changed, utterly.

No, he decided. These emotions, if they were ever to be addressed, would, as William said, take time to emerge; long periods of circumspect conversation and guarded revelation. What mattered most now was trust.

"Did you drink too much as well?"

"Catherine, do you still love me?"

The question shocked them both. "What?" she asked, then was silent for a few moments. "Yes, John. I love you."

"I had this feeling that you don't . . . don't trust me. That you'd spent the night with someone else." As he said it, he cringed and writhed within.

"Me? No. Look, John. No way. I . . . I admit I was angry you'd gone off again."

"You thought I was seeing someone else."

"What?" she said again with a tone of genuine confusion. He could imagine the wrinkling of her brow, the tilt of her head. "Seeing someone?"

Now that he had started, he had to carry on. "You're always upset when I go away. You think I'm cheating on you."

"No," she said emphatically. "No way. I do not think that. John, you've imagined that. I don't think you're cheating on me. Are you?"

"Of course not. But there's something wrong. You're angry about something."

She paused for some time. He listened to her breathing. From her end of the line he could hear the television, a cartoon. Brandon would be sat in front of it, his red Wellington boots on, eyes wide and fixed on the screen. When she spoke again her voice had softened. It was the pitch of someone carefully broaching a delicate issue.

"I don't know. Yes. I'm angry when you go away. I just wonder sometimes if all this is worth it. You know? The weekends away. The book. I mean, I don't want to see you put all this effort into the ghost thing for nothing."

He had not heard his before. This was a novelty and it took him by surprise.

"If it's worth it?"

"The time you spend on it."

Up until that morning, although he would never have admitted it, John may have agreed with her. There was a desperation about his work that he was unwilling to face. The launch of the book terrified him and he often wished he had never written it. But that was before the events of the previous night. Things had changed.

"This isn't the time," she said. "We can't do this on the phone."

"No."

"I love you, John. Come home."

"Yes."

He returned to the dining room and sat heavily at his table. He stared at his plate. When she finished tidying, Susan came and sat with him, poured herself a coffee.

"So," she began, tipping sugar into her cup, "the underground passage is responsible for the haunting. Is that right?"

He studied her face to see if she was alluding to any of the revelations her husband had shared.

"That's where the infrasound is coming from. There's a waterfall under the building, the noise of it is channelled and amplified by the tunnel."

She stirred the sugar into her black coffee, slow and deliberate, tapped the teaspoon twice on the cup's rim, and lifted it to drink. Her lips that morning were a darkish pink, there was a lighter hue on her eyelids. She was wearing a dark green dress with a faint ivy pattern and a pale orange scarf. Her hair, perhaps recently brushed, seemed bigger, thicker. Her beauty was bright and clear and shone through the fog in his brain.

"You really could be the reincarnation of one of those women in the paintings in the bar," he said, quite before he realised what he was saying.

She nodded and gave a little shake of her hair. "William's very fond of his pre-Raphaelites."

"The prints are his?"

"Oh yes. I match them, not the other way around. I'm the latest in a long line of similar-looking women. I think I've lasted a bit longer than most, though. I guess he's slowing down."

They drank their coffee. John picked crumbs from the tablecloth and dropped them onto his plate. When he looked at her again, she smiled at him. He felt he was being commiserated in some way.

"I can make the haunting go away," he said at long last.

Her scepticism was signalled by the way her eyebrows raised. She finished her coffee and stared into the cup.

"I can do it," he affirmed.

She sighed and lifted her head. "Please, do try."

By the time the Lisbeth and Matt were back at the inn, John was ready to finish the job. He set up his laptop, connected the multidirectional mike, and the slender peak of the 19Hz appeared onscreen. Another piece of wood was cut and shaped to the measurements he had made. Earlier, whilst poking around in the shed, he had discovered some foam-filled cushions from an old sofa, and these he requisitioned. His final request was for a power drill, Rawlplugs, and screws. When all was ready, William and Susan were asked to join them. John disappeared down the hole with the materials he had collected. He wedged the cushions in front of the iron bars so that they blocked the mouth of the tunnel, then used the piece of wood to further seal the opening. With the drill, he bored four holes into the rock, and screwed the wood tightly into place.

On climbing out, he could see by the others' faces that a change had taken place. One look at the laptop confirmed it. The infrasound had been shut off.

The owners were wide-eyed. Lisbeth photographed everyone.

When it was time to leave, John was invited to come back for a free weekend's accommodation.

"And you'll bring your family, yes?" asked William, gripping his hand.

"Sounds lovely. I know my wife could do with a holiday."

Susan kissed his cheek. She smiled warmly. "Thank you, John. For everything."

As Matt drove them out onto the road, John waved from the back seat.

"What a crazy weekend," said Lisbeth turning back to face front. "We should do it again sometime."

John slept for most of the journey to London.

He was dropped off at the end of his street. Matt said he would be in touch; Lisbeth promised to email him some of her photos. Then they were gone.

There had been heavy rain in the city over the weekend; large pools of dirty water lingered over blocked drains, lapping the kerb every time a car went by. The pavements were an autumnal patchwork of sodden leaves.

It was nearly six in the evening and the sky was dark. As he neared his flat he could see lights in the first floor living room windows. He imagined the scene inside: Catherine would be going over notes for the week ahead, perhaps her first glass of wine on the table next to her. Brandon, out of the bath, cosy in pyjamas and dressing gown, damp hair smelling like sweets, reading his favourite comic for the hundredth time. John knew he would take the boy in his arms when he got in, hold him tight and make him squirm and complain he was being squashed. And he would kiss Catherine and tell her that he loved her, and only her, and let her know how thankful he was they had found each other.

An evening in with the family. A good dinner, wine, perhaps a film later. Work in the morning, but that was okay. His tongue, in what had become a habit, ran across the troublesome tooth, and he made a mental note to arrange a visit to the dentist.

Somewhere nearby a siren wailed, as if to say, welcome back, this is the city and you belong here. The streetlights blinked on, orange and dull, brightening by degrees.

John turned the key, opened the front door, and went inside.

ACKNOWLEDGEMENTS

I wish to thank John Huntington, Professor of Entertainment Technology at New York City College of Technology, for his help with the technicalities of infrasound.

Find out more about his work at www.controlgeek.net.

I also wish to acknowledge the work of the late Vic Tandy who was the first to link infrasonic events with hauntings. His 1998 paper, "The Ghost in the Machine," written with Tony R. Lawrence, is a fascinating introduction to the field.

ABOUT THE AUTHOR

Simon Kearns grew up in the North of Ireland and now lives in the South of France. His short stories have appeared in a variety of publications and on numerous websites. He is fascinated by etymology, Neolithic Europe, and the workings of the news media. His debut novel, *Virtual Assassin*, was published by Revenge Ink in 2010.